WED FOR A WAGER

Grace Hadley must enter into a marriage of convenience with handsome young Rupert Shalford, otherwise Sir John, her step-father, will sell her to the highest bidder. But Rupert's older brother Lord Ralph Shalford has other ideas and is determined he will have the union dissolved. However, Sir John is equally determined to recover his now missing step-daughter. Will Grace ever find the happiness she deserves?

FENELLA MILLER

WED FOR A WAGER

Complete and Unabridged

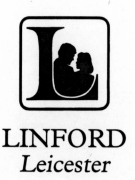

LINFORD
Leicester

First published in Great Britain in 2012

First Linford Edition
published 2013

A catalogue record for this book is available
from the British Library.

ISBN 978–1–4448–1577–1

Published by
F. A. Thorpe (Publishing)
Anstey, Leicestershire

Set by Words & Graphics Ltd.
Anstey, Leicestershire
Printed and bound in Great Britain by
T. J. International Ltd., Padstow, Cornwall

This book is printed on acid-free paper

Plotting An Escape

Grace checked a second time that her door was locked. Loud voices were approaching her chamber.

'It ain't right, Radcliffe, allowing your daughter to hide from us. You promised her to the highest bidder. That's me.'

'Look here, Bennett, it won't do any good chasing about up here. I've given you my permission to try your luck, that don't mean it'll be easy persuading the wretched girl to agree to marry you.'

Grace pressed closer to the door; she needed to hear exactly what her pernicious step-father was planning. If she was to have any chance of remaining safe when his cronies were in residence, she must be forewarned.

'I ain't going to take no for an answer. If she won't come willing, then I'll do it the other way.'

'She'll come round in time. I tell you, you'll not coerce her easily. She takes after her father, a colonel in the Horse Guards and famous for his quick temper and stubbornness.'

'That's as may be, Radcliffe, but I ain't marrying her for her temperament nor her looks, but for half her dowry.'

The door rattled on its hinges. Grace froze. She held her breath and waited. The smell of alcohol seeped through the cracks of the door.

Sir John spoke. 'Come away, Bennett, she'll not come out. Since her mother died she makes herself scarce. Used to be a pretty little thing, but she's gone downhill these past two years.'

The two men stumbled back down the passageway, their feet heavy on the boards. Her breath hissed through her teeth and she pushed the heavy oak settle against the door. She felt safer with both the key turned and a piece of furniture in place to prevent unwanted visitors.

Since she'd taken residence in the

rooms on the nursery floor previously occupied by her governess, she had been able to keep away from the predatory gentleman who frequently prowled around Hadley Manor. Before her mother passed away she suggested Grace dye her hair with walnut juice and adopt the costume of a spinster aunt. In this way one became almost invisible, no-one noticed a plain woman. She'd almost forgotten what her original colour had been, but Mama had often likened it to the colour of autumn leaves.

She no longer had her own maid as Sir John wished to make her uncomfortable in the hope he might persuade her to marry one of his repellent friends. Never! She would rather die. The clothes she wore nowadays needed no abigail's assistance. Poor Molly was working as a parlour maid but that was better than being turned off without a reference.

Tonight had confirmed her worst fears. Sir John was an inveterate gambler and was permanently in debt, relying on what he could trick out of the lawyers who controlled her trust fund. Marrying her to one of his friends would mean he could demand a large settlement.

She must get away. How could she persuade him to allow her to leave? Perhaps there was something she could do to save herself. Isobel Cunningham had written only last week to invite Grace to live with her. If she told Sir John she was going to visit an old school friend he might allow her to go.

Tonight she would write a letter accepting the invitation and see that Molly took it down to the posting inn first thing. That night Grace slept more soundly than she had for months and woke quite refreshed.

Mr Bennett would still be abed, but her step-father would be up and about. He was an early riser. However much he had imbibed he would appear for breakfast at nine o'clock exactly every morning. Grace usually ate in her room but today she would go and talk to him.

Holding the letter from Isobel in her hand she hurried downstairs to the breakfast parlour. She paused outside the door to steady her breathing then stepped through.

Sir John looked up, his red cheeks bulging with food. He was unable to answer until he swallowed but gestured that Grace be seated in the chair opposite. The footman, hovering by the sideboard, hastily filled her plate with random samples from the silver chafing dishes. She stared in dismay at coddled eggs, ham, strawberry conserve and toasted teacakes haphazardly presented on the same plate.

If she hadn't been so nervous she would have smiled. She would speak her piece at once for he couldn't shout at her with his mouth full.

'Sir John, I beg your pardon for joining you here this morning but I have a request to make. Yesterday I received a letter from an old school friend inviting me to stay for a week or two.' She waved the paper about. 'I should dearly like to visit if you would kindly give me permission.'

He slammed his cutlery down on either side of his piled plate and leaned towards her, his pale blue eyes bulging horribly. 'I'll let you go on one condition. When you get back you must choose from one of the offers you've received.'

Schooling her features was difficult, but somehow she managed to keep her dismay from showing. 'I scarcely know any of the gentlemen, I have no wish to tie myself to a stranger or one old enough to be my father.'

'Whose fault is that? You never join us, and skulk around like a servant. But there is someone you've yet to meet, Reginald Bennett, he's looking for a wife to take care of his motherless children.'

'I see. I love children, as you know. Tell me a little about this gentleman, if you please, Sir John.' She clutched her napkin and waited to hear what lies would spill from his mouth.

'He's in his thirties, a fine figure of a man, not given to gambling or drinking. He's searching for a girl who will love his children as his sainted wife did, and I reckon you will be perfect for each other.'

It would not do to appear over-enthusiastic; her stepfather would immediately suspect she was dissembling. 'He sounds far more suitable than the other gentlemen you have suggested. Where does he live?'

'Hertfordshire or Hereford, don't remember which. Anyway, he's got a neat little estate, a fine manor house which will no doubt be improved by having a wife to take control of things once more.'

'I give you my word I will consider his offer seriously when I return from my visit to St Albans. If he's the man you describe, then he might well suit me admirably.'

'Very well, miss, you may go. But for no more than two weeks. Now, if you ain't going to eat your breakfast be about your business; I wish to finish mine without your sour face watching.'

Grace didn't need telling a second time. Delighted to be sent away she pushed back her chair and curtsied before hurrying out. She had difficulty keeping her delight from showing. Her plan had worked perfectly; she had two weeks in which to come up with a scheme to remove herself permanently from Hadley Manor.

She spotted Molly industriously dusting in the drawing-room and slipped inside to speak to her. 'I'm to go and visit Mrs Cunningham in Romford and I will have you reassigned to me.'

'Thank you, miss. Will I continue with my duties here or come at once to your apartment?'

It would be better not to give Bloomfield, the recently appointed housekeeper, an opportunity to refuse the request. If Molly was already re-established as her abigail the wretched woman would have to accept the change.

'Please go at once to your room and collect your belongings, Molly. I wish you to move into the nursery maid's room adjacent to mine immediately. I'm going to walk over to Bracken Hall, it might be better if you came with me.'

By the time Grace had changed into an outmoded, but far more flattering ensemble, Molly was bustling about next door. Marianne Duncan, her best friend, understood the reason Grace wished to seem drab and unattractive, but her parents were not party to the deception. Therefore when she visited her she concealed her hideous hair under a pretty chip-straw bonnet and dressed appropriately for a young woman of means.

As usual she kept to the back stairs and exited the house through a little-used side door. The distance was no more than a mile across the fields and the early April weather perfect for walking. Molly trotted respectfully behind, she knew better than to engage her mistress in idle chatter.

On arrival at her destination Grace ignored the imposing front door; she did her best to avoid any interaction with Mr and Mrs Duncan. The less they knew of her life the better. Her friend would still be at her toilette, an ideal time for intimate conversation. Molly and the girl who took care of Marianne were firm friends and would be pleased to spend an hour or two together.

She reached Marianne's chambers and tapped lightly. Hurrying footsteps approached.

'Grace, how lovely to see you. It's been ages since you walked over. What brings you here so early?' Her blonde curls danced on either side of her face. 'Have you any more to tell me about the dreadful men Sir John is parading in front of you this year?'

'I do, indeed. I have something of the utmost urgency to discuss with you. Perhaps you could breakfast in your parlour this morning and I might join you? I am sharp set, my appetite has returned.'

'Life here would be so dull if I did not have your exciting tales of dreadful debauchery and bad behaviour.'

Much as she adored her best friend, she had an unfortunate tendency to the melodramatic. Grace dreaded to think what Mr and Mrs Duncan would do if they ever heard the much-embellished version of her life that Marianne preferred to believe was the truth.

'I do wish you would not exaggerate, my dear. My life is difficult enough without the added worry of your parents believing I am living in a house of ill repute.'

Marianne giggled and embraced her friend. 'Dearest, I never said any such thing. But you know me, I have to add an extra detail or two to any story I hear.'

Once they were comfortably settled Grace explained her predicament. 'So, I have gained myself two weeks. However, I've no idea how to avoid being married to Mr Bennett on my return.'

'Could you not find yourself a position as a governess? You're so clever, can speak French and Italian like a native, play the pianoforte, and your stitching and watercolours are exemplary.'

'Believe me, I have considered that option; but I should require a reference or at the very least a letter of good character. I can hardly ask Mr Colley next time I attend church, for my step-father would hear of it immediately.'

The conversation was interrupted as Molly and Sarah carried in the breakfast tray. Once they were private again her friend came up with a remarkable suggestion. 'You must contract a marriage of convenience; you reached your majority last year so do not need Sir John's permission.'

'An excellent notion, my love, but I am unlikely to find a suitable husband in the next three weeks. Consider this, who in their right mind would contract such a marriage? Looking as I do and dressed in outmoded fashions, I doubt all but the most desperate of men would give me a second glance and they would hardly be ready to tie the knot immediately.'

'It hardly matters what you look like, as it will be a marriage in name only. I shall write to Lucy Pearson, she moves in the highest circles and will know exactly the right gentleman to approach . . . '

Grace laughed. 'Enough of this nonsense; I would no sooner marry a stranger than I would any of the repellent gentlemen my step-father has brought down. I shall remain with Isobel. Far better to be an unpaid companion than the alternative you suggest.'

'I suppose I'm not to write to Lucy?'

'Of course not; I do appreciate your kind thoughts but would much prefer you did not become involved.'

Her friend shrugged and took another swallow from her bowl of chocolate. 'Very well, but I shall give the matter some thought. I'm quite certain I read of exactly such a thing in one of the novels I obtained from the library recently.'

'What I do need is to borrow some money for my journey. Sir John will only give me sufficient funds to reach St Albans. I shall need extra in order to get to Romford and this journey will include an overnight stay.'

'How exciting! I do so wish I could have an adventure like that, life is so boring here. I think Papa was grossly unfair to forbid me a season this year just because I attempted to elope with Lt. Blackwell.' She jumped to her feet, scattering cutlery and crumbs in all directions. 'I'm sure I have several guineas in my reticule. You shall have it all; I do hope it will be enough.'

Marianne emptied her bag on the table and gold coins rolled in all directions.

'Good heavens! There must be at least five guineas here. Are you sure you can spare it all?' Grace gathered up the money and stacked it tidily on the tablecloth.

'Yes, take it. Papa is generous with my pin money and will replace it when I ask. Please don't worry about repaying me as you will need every penny if you are to set out on your own.' She frowned. 'I don't suppose even five guineas will be enough to last until you are five and twenty for that is more than three years.'

'You are a wonderful friend, I shall miss you sorely. Fond as I am of Isobel she does not have a sunny disposition like you.' Grace hugged her friend and blinked away the tears. If only Mama had not been bamboozled into marriage by Sir John life would be so different now.

On her return to Hadley Manor she was unseen and slipped inside. She was safely upstairs before setting her plan in motion. 'Molly, you must pack my trunk and then go to the Red Lion and book us two seats on the mail coach for

St Albans. I shall pen a letter to Mrs Cunningham and you can send that at the same time.'

'When are we leaving, miss?'

Grace considered. It would take at least a day for the letter to reach Isobel in Romford and two days for her to receive a reply. 'Reserve places for Monday morning — there is a coach that departs at eight o'clock. We will have to make our way across the town to The King's Head in order to take the coach to Romford. We shall overnight in London and complete our journey the following day.'

Molly curtsied and disappeared into the small antechamber Grace had been using as her dressing-room. This letter was a difficult task; she hated to be beholden to anyone and knew that Isobel's invitation was not quite what it seemed. Well aware that life was becoming intolerable at Hadley Manor, her old school friend had offered a home in exchange for working as an unpaid companion.

She folded the letter and sealed the edge neatly with a blob of wax. Molly put her head around the door, her cap askew and her apron sadly wrinkled.

'Miss Hadley, am I putting everything in or leaving the nasty brown clothes behind?'

'The only items that fit me are the brown ones; the others hang disastrously both back and front.' She stared at the pretty promenade dress she was wearing. This was the only garment from her previous life that had been altered to fit. 'Pack any gowns it will be possible to alter. We shall not have the wherewithal to buy new material. Are you quite sure you wish to accompany me to what will certainly be a life of drudgery?'

'Yes, miss, as long as I am by your side I shall be content.'

'I'm glad to hear you say so, Molly. My letter is finished; please take it to the post inn right away. The packing can wait for we shall not be leaving just yet.'

Four days passed and still there was no word from Isobel. Grace hovered anxiously in the shrubbery in the hope that she might waylay the delivery just in case the butler decided to keep the missive until Sir John returned.

'There you are, Grace, I thought I saw you lurking in the bushes. The most amazing thing has happened, I had to come at once and tell you.'

'I wish you hadn't, Marianne, it would have been far better to have sent a message for me to come to you. Quickly, come inside before you are seen and attract unwanted attention.'

Grace grabbed her friend's arm and bundled her around to the side of the house and into the door. She whisked her into the schoolroom. Breathless she embraced Marianne. 'I do beg your pardon for my abruptness, dearest, but you know how things are at Hadley Manor. Although Sir John is away from home for a few days, he still has his spies watching out for everything I do or say.'

Her companion stepped back, her eyes sparkling. Grace's heart dropped to her boots; such an expression always meant Marianne had done something outrageous.

Shalford Hall

Ralph rubbed his eyes and tossed his pen down on the desk. The clock had stuck twelve; high time he turned in. Digby, his valet, must be anxious to get to his own bed. A hesitant tap on the study door startled him.

'Enter.'

The butler, Foster, stepped inside and bowed. 'Lord Shalford, I beg your pardon for disturbing you, but there is . . . there is an incident in the village that requires your attention.'

'What now? Does this mysterious event involve my brother?'

'I'm afraid that it does, my lord.'

'Is the carriage ready? Have you sent for Evans and Digby?'

'I have, my lord, they are waiting in the vestibule.'

Ralph strode through the Hall, grateful that at least the evening was clement and he would not have to put on his topcoat or gloves before departing. He gestured to the two men hovering by the front door and they trooped after him. A closed carriage was standing outside, the team of four matched bays eager to be done with this escapade.

The carriage rocked as he climbed in, Evans and Digby caused less movement. Being so large was a damnable nuisance and unbalancing the carriage was the least of it. 'Have you any idea what my brother has done this time?' He addressed the remark to the far side of the carriage; one or other of the men would have the information he wanted.

Evans cleared his throat. 'It would appear, my lord, Mr Rupert is in his cups and, urged on by his friend, has decided to pay his addresses to Miss Ashley.'

This was the last time his younger brother would embarrass him. He had been too lenient, had paid his gambling debts and extricated him from several unfortunate liaisons — but enough was definitely enough. From now on his younger brother would have his allowance curtailed until he came to his senses. Rupert must live a blemish-free life and not continue to cause their beloved mother so much pain. He should have stepped in sooner but since Mama's accident he had been loath to upset her by curbing the excesses of her favourite son.

The carriage completed the journey in a quarter of an hour. Ralph jumped from the vehicle without waiting for the steps to be lowered. Thank God all was quiet outside the vicarage, no lights on in the house and no crowd of disapproving villagers gawping at his brother's latest tomfoolery.

He stood listening. Yes, he could hear voices further down the lane. As he walked briskly towards the two indistinct shapes, Ralph became more incensed with each step he took. He was heartily sick of being dragged from his bed to attend to this young puppy's misdemeanours or being obliged to go to town in order to settle his brother's debts.

Fortunately there was sufficient moonlight to see without the necessity of taking the lanterns from the coach. 'Rupert, enough of this nonsense. Bid your friend good night and come with me.'

His brother staggered against the tall brick wall and stared blearily at him. 'Ralph, what you doing here? Come to help me wake up my future bride?'

Ignoring his equally inebriated companion Ralph stepped up and gripped Rupert's arm. 'No, you fool, I've come to take you home before you make a bigger fool of yourself than usual.'

'But Jack says Miss Ashley smiled at me when we passed in the street this afternoon. Must mean she likes me, don't you see?'

'No doubt she did, for some reason the fair sex find you an attractive fellow. However, that's no excuse for larking about in the middle of the night.'

Allowing his brother no room for manoeuvre he took one elbow and Evans took the other. Together they marched him to the carriage where Digby was waiting to pull him in.

By the time the coachman had turned the vehicle Rupert was snoring loudly in the corner. His sibling was a constant trial but he loved him dearly. His lips curved as he recalled the day his parents had called him into Mama's bedchamber. He had been almost ten years of age, as pleased with the new arrival as they had been.

Rupert's nature was affectionate and he was universally adored. He thrived on the attention and looked up to his big brother, especially after their papa had died from an apoplexy some years ago. Perhaps if his brother had been more firmly disciplined he would not have turned out the way he had. He was mixing with a rackety crew whose influence was not beneficial on one lacking in maturity and common sense. Thank the good Lord, Rupert would not have access to his inheritance until he was twenty-five, unless he married before that date.

Ralph jerked upright. So that was why Simmons had tried to persuade his brother to pay his addresses to the vicar's daughter. The leeches who had attached themselves to Rupert were after a share of his fortune. If Rupert got himself a wife he would be his own master and able to dispose of his money as he wished.

*   *   *

Grim faced, Ralph awaited the appearance of his brother in his study. The time was already past noon and there was still no sign of him. He had promised Mama he would go upstairs after the interview and tell her what had been decided. Noisy footsteps in the corridor announced the arrival of his errant sibling. Not bothering to knock, Rupert barged in, his eyes bloodshot and his expression belligerent.

'Well, let's get it over with. I don't want a bear-garden jaw, I can tell you. My head's thumping like a drum.'

'And a good morning to you, brother. I have ordered strong coffee to be brought; sit down, and stop scowling like a recalcitrant schoolboy.'

Rupert almost grinned as he dropped heavily into the chair on the opposite side of the desk. 'I don't appreciate being dragged out of bed by my valet. If Evans weren't so useful I'd give him his marching orders.'

The rattle of crockery heralded the arrival of the much-needed aromatic brew.

Ralph waved away the footman, preferring to pour the coffee himself. Cook had also sent a selection of pastries, scones and bread-and-butter. No point in offering Rupert anything to eat, after one of his heavy drinking sessions his digestion was in turmoil for several days.

Ralph helped himself to bread-and-butter and cup of coffee before resuming his seat. He waited until his brother looked up before speaking again. 'Rupert, last night's nonsense was the outside of enough. You are twenty-one, it is high time you gave up your roistering and your ill-advised cronies. Can you imagine the furore you would have made if I had not prevented you from hammering on Mr Ashley's door last night? What were you thinking of? You have overstepped the mark this time, and I shall not allow it to continue.'

His brother scowled. 'I'm not a child, Ralph, and I won't be dictated to by anyone. I've reached my majority and shall do as I please — there's nothing you can do to prevent it.'

'You forget, brother, that I hold the purse strings. You have no choice. If you don't live within your means then you are on your own. I shall pay no more of your debts; unless you retire to your estate in Essex and behave responsibly your bills will remain unpaid.'

Rupert surged to his feet, sending his

chair crashing backwards. 'I'll do as I please. I'm going back to town tonight. There's a horse race in Cheapside and I've already wagered fifty guineas on the outcome.'

'Don't go off in high dudgeon. I have your best interests at heart; I don't want you to destroy your health and happiness by dissolute living.' Ralph's fingers clenched on the arm of his chair. Using his unnatural size to intimidate his sibling was not an option. He would drive the boy away and that was the last thing he wanted.

'You're a killjoy, Ralph. You don't want to have any fun yourself, can't even find yourself a bride, so have nothing better to do with your time than ruin my life.' He turned and kicked the chair aside before stomping off, slamming the door loudly behind him.

With a sigh Ralph sank back in his seat. He had made a sad mull of things, exacerbated the situation instead of improving it. He'd offered to buy the boy his colours last year but this had been thrown back in his face. He should never have listened to their mother. When the boy had wanted to join the cavalry he should have allowed it. His brother was at far greater risk in England than he would be on the Continent. With Napoleon safely locked up on Elba there were no battles to be fought which was possibly why his brother no longer wished to join.

He had the unpleasant duty of informing Mama that not only had Rupert not apologised for his reprehensible behaviour, he had ignored the warnings about his allowance being cut off. Convincing her that he was being cruel to be kind was going to be difficult. Letting Rupert accumulate debts, become unpopular with his creditors, was the only way to persuade his brother to give up his reckless ways.

He munched his way through several scones and strawberry conserve and emptied the coffee jug before he felt ready to go upstairs. When his mother had taken a crushing fall the previous-year and severely damaged her back the specialist from London had been certain she would eventually regain strength in her legs and be able to walk. However this had not happened; the months passed and his beloved parent remained marooned in her apartment, seemingly no nearer recovering than she had been before Christmas.

His mother looked up, her face sad. 'My dear, don't look so worried. I'm well aware what took place both last night and today. Nothing remains a secret for very long.' She patted the at the end of the chaise longue. 'Come and sit down, tell me what you decided.'

He bent down and kissed her still golden hair. 'He stormed off, as usual, ignoring everything I said to him. I'm afraid, Mama, this time I'm determined to stick to my word. I will not be cajoled or wheedled into paying his debts or rescuing him from any scrapes.'

'And neither should you, my love. It's high time Rupert understood his wild behaviour has consequences not only for himself, but also for those who love him. I'm quite sure a spell in a debtor's prison would do him good.'

'I shall not let it come to that.' His mother's gurgle of laughter broke the tension. 'You are an insufferable tease, Mama, and I should not let myself be taken in.'

'I know you too well, dear boy. For all his faults, and I'm the first to admit he has many, he has no malice in him and will soon come to his senses. His fair-weather friends will desert him if he has no gold in his pockets. Then he will see we were right and come home to straighten himself out.'

'In which case, Mama, you must both pray he does nothing too foolhardy before his luck runs out.'

Hadley Manor

Grace waited whilst her friend removed her bonnet and gloves. 'Well, Marianne, what is it that has brought you here in such a flurry?'

'I have received a letter from Lydia Banister. You remember her? She was in the year below us at the seminary? Well, her brother is a great friend of Mr Simmons and a young man called Rupert Shalford.'

Grace was becoming more puzzled by the moment. 'What have these gentlemen to do with me?'

'I was coming to that, Grace. It seems Mr Shalford is in a similar position to you; he wishes to contract a marriage of convenience immediately. His brother, Lord Shalford, is a cruel monster and is denying him his rightful inheritance. The only way he can access his own money is by marrying. He has reached his majority and needs no permission.'

'My dear Marianne, this sounds like a tale from one of your more lurid romances.' A horrible sinking feeling developed in the pit of her stomach. 'Tell me you have not spoken of my situation to complete strangers? I could not bear it if you have done so.'

Her friend blushed scarlet. 'I might have mentioned it in passing. I can assure you Lydia is the soul of discretion.'

'So discreet that she discussed the fact you have a friend seeking a suitable husband with a friend of her brother?' Grace was tempted to throw a book at Marianne but sensibly refrained. 'It will be all over the county by the end of the week. I shall be ruined and Sir John will be justifiably incensed.'

'Oh no, it will not come to that,' was the airy reply. 'I have all the necessary information about Mr Shalford. All you have to do is decide if he is the sort of person you could think of marrying.

I'm sure in a year or two you could have the marriage dissolved or annulled or something of that sort.'

The paper was held out and reluctantly Grace took it. She quickly scanned the contents: Mr Shalford was the youngest son of a peer; he was twenty-one, had an estate in Essex and sufficient funds to keep a wife and live comfortably.

Her pulse quickened. Was this the miracle she'd prayed for? Lydia Banister seemed an unlikely conduit through which the Almighty might work, but stranger things did happen.

'Are you sure these details are correct? That Mr Shalford is in a similar position to me and is only contracting a marriage of convenience to remove himself from the control of his unpleasant brother?'

Marianne clapped her hands. 'Everything is accurate, I have Lydia's word. Are you going to meet Mr Shalford?'

'If he can be at The King's Head in St Albans the day after tomorrow then I shall meet him to discuss the matter. I'm not so desperate I will marry without first meeting my future husband. If I cannot like him, even though it will be in name only, I shall not consent, but continue on my way to Isobel Cunningham's home in Romford.'

'I cannot believe you are about to embark on such a romantic adventure, Grace. Is there anything else I can do for you before I leave? I didn't tell Mama I was coming here and she might be anxious about my absence.'

'No, dearest friend, I shall be for ever in your debt. I must write a reply to Mr Shalford at his London address and pray he receives it in time. I shall also ask him to arrange for a curate to marry us and to obtain the special licence.'

'I believe one can obtain such a document in town. I must ride through the village on my way home so I will delay for a few more minutes whilst you write your letter then I can send it for you. It must go express, you know, to ensure it arrives in good time.'

Twenty minutes later Marianne had departed with the letter and Grace explained to Molly what her new plans were. They were not received well.

'Miss Hadley, whatever were you thinking of? If you will pardon me for saying so, Miss Duncan is of a romantic nature and not the most practical young lady. How can you be sure you're not stepping from one problem into another?'

'I am not committing myself to anything before I meet Mr Shalford. If I decide not to proceed then I shall continue on my way to Romford and things will be as before. I have nothing to lose and possibly everything to gain.'

Molly shook her head. 'Then I had best complete your packing. Shall I leave out the gown I altered for you, the one with the matching spencer and bonnet?'

'No, I think it best that I travel as inconspicuously as possible. A lady alone on a stage could be the subject of unpleasant attention from male passengers. However I shall wear it if I do decide to marry Mr Shalford.'

The very idea was quite nonsensical, but for the first time since her mother had died her spirits were high. Finally she had something to look forward to.

★ ★ ★

The journey to St Albans was uneventful. Grace had no difficulty discovering the direction of The King's Head. The inn was but a short step from the hostelry at which she had alighted. She spoke to the landlord and arranged for her trunk to be transported to The King's Head leaving her maid to manage the smaller bags.

'We have arrived in good time, Molly, and should have no difficulty reserving a room for tonight. I wonder if Mr Shalford has also arrived.'

Her maid shifted a carpet bag under her arm before answering. 'Didn't he say the time you were to meet, Miss Hadley?'

'Indeed he did; he was most precise

with his instructions. We are to rendezvous in a private parlour at exactly four o'clock. We are to spend an hour together before deciding if we wish to proceed. You will remain with me at all times, of course, Molly.'

'Yes, miss, I'll not let you out of my sight. If you decide to go ahead, when will the ceremony take place?'

'At six o'clock. Then we shall dine together and retire to our separate chambers. Tomorrow we shall depart for his estate in Essex where our lawyers will attend us to arrange for the release of our funds.'

Speaking the words out loud made it all seem horribly real. What was she thinking of? How could she be contemplating entering the holy state of matrimony when she had no intention of honouring, obeying, and certainly not begetting. To be about to marry a complete stranger for mercenary reasons, however pressing these were, was beginning to seem very wrong.

'Here we are. I shall go at once and

speak to the landlord.' Grace walked into the dim interior of the ancient building. The beamed ceiling would be a hazard to anyone above average height. There was a stout wooden table at the far end of the spacious vestibule upon which rested a large brass bell. Molly dropped the three bags and hurried across to ring it.

A tall, spare woman of middle years hurried out from the passageway and stood behind the table. She was dressed from top to toe in dark blue cotton, a spotless white apron around her middle and a remarkably pretty lace cap on her head.

'Good morning, miss, can I be of assistance? Mrs Turnbull is my name, I am the landlady here.'

'Good morning. My name is Miss Hadley and I'd like a room for tonight with a separate parlour. I also require a truckle bed for my abigail.'

'I have an apartment which will suit you perfectly. It is at the back of the building and very quiet. Will you be requiring supper in your room?'

'No thank you, Mrs Turnbull, I shall be dining with another of your guests who has already reserved a private parlour.'

Grace felt the blood flood into her cheeks. Good heavens! It must sound as if she had a clandestine assignation and was a young woman of dubious morals. The landlady pursed her lips.

'Very well, Miss Hadley. I shall have hot water sent to your rooms immediately. Shall you be requiring anything else?' Her tone was decidedly frosty

'No, thank you. I shall leave my maid to take care of the formalities. Kindly show me to my chamber.' She had been going to request luncheon be sent but she had lost her appetite. She waited with as much dignity as she could muster for a boot boy to be summoned to carry the bags and escort her upstairs.

The rooms allocated to her were more than adequate. A parlour adjoined the bedchamber and there was a small anteroom in which the truckle bed for Molly could be set up.

'Put the bags in the bedchamber, if you please.' The boy did she as she bid, tugged his forelock and vanished.

Molly puffed in behind her. 'My, this is far better than I expected. It's clean and the sheets freshly starched. Nothing to complain of here.'

The hot water arrived and whilst Molly put out the recently altered gown Grace stripped off the hated brown dress. With the grime of the journey rinsed from her person she was refreshed and a little calmer. 'I have yet to cancel our seats on the stage for tomorrow, I thought it better to wait until . . . well . . . to wait until later.'

'Shall I put your hair up in a more becoming style, miss? We can't do anything about the colour, and the walnut juice makes it dull and lifeless, but with a bit of ribbon I reckon I can make it more pleasing.'

She was tempted to refuse. The last thing she wanted to do was appear an attractive proposition to this young man. After she spoke her vows, whatever her wishes, she would be legally bound to him. 'No, I think it best I don't wear my sprigged muslin. I'll keep it for tomorrow. Either I shall be starting a new life as Mrs Shalford and will want to look my best or will be continuing my journey to live with Mrs Cunningham. In either case I don't want to look like a governess.'

An hour later she was regretting her decision not to send for refreshments. 'Molly, can you go down and see if you can find us something to eat? It's still three hours until I am to go downstairs to dine with Mr Shalford.'

The few moments later there was a sharp knock on the door. Botheration! Molly must have both hands occupied and needed the door opening for her. She uncurled her feet from beneath her, put aside her book and stepped across to open the door. She clutched the wall for support. A startlingly handsome young man stood framed in the doorway.

'Miss Hadley, I beg your pardon for arriving unannounced but I could not wait a moment longer to meet you.' The gentleman bowed and his corn-coloured locks tumbled across his brow. 'Rupert Shalford at your service.'

Recovering her self-composure with difficulty, Grace curtsied. 'Mr Shalford, I cannot invite you in as my maid is elsewhere. However, I would be happy to join you downstairs for some luncheon.'

His blue eyes held hers for a disturbing moment. 'I shall order a meal directly.' He delved into his jacket pocket and produced a sheaf of folded paper. 'Here, Miss Hadley, I thought you might like to read these letters from my lawyers before you make your decision.'

'Thank you, sir, I'm sorry but I don't have a similar package for you. However I have written down all I know about my trust fund myself. I hope that's acceptable?' Glad to be away from someone so attractive she hurried to her reticule and withdrew the required papers. This was one thing she hadn't thought to ask about her prospective husband. It had not occurred to her he might be a desirable partner. Thank goodness she had remained in her unattractive gown with her hair scraped back.

She thrust the document into his hand. 'Here you are, Mr Shalford. I shall join you downstairs in half an hour. That should give us time to peruse the contents.'

He grinned, nodded absently, and sauntered off whistling a jaunty tune. She read sufficient to understand she was not making a misalliance. Mr Shalford was well-connected, well-respected by his lawyers and was as wealthy as she had been told. The only drawback to the arrangement was the fact he was so personable.

Her lips curved. Would it be so very bad if they fell in love and the marriage became a genuine arrangement? Annoyed by her romantic nonsense she re-folded the papers and put them inside the novel she was reading. Her thoughts were better suited to Marianne, Grace had always prided herself on being of a practical nature and not given to the fanciful notions of her friend.

When Molly staggered in bearing a laden tray she was ready to leave. 'I'm so sorry, Molly, but I'm to eat with Mr Shalford. Put the tray somewhere cool and cover it with a damp cloth; I'm sure it will keep for your supper.' Not allowing her garrulous abigail to comment she collected her reticule and headed for the vestibule. Molly trundled along behind her muttering under her breath.

There was no need to ask for directions to the parlour as Mr Shalford bounded out from a door a little way along the left-hand passageway. 'I say, Miss Hadley, down here. I'm sharp set, I've not eaten since last night.' His voice boomed along the panelled walls, startling an unfortunate pot-boy who slopped ale down his apron.

Grace dashed towards her host hoping to prevent him calling out her name so loudly a second time. 'Mr Shalford, it might be better if we left the door ajar.'

'No, we must close it. Don't want our business overheard.' He grabbed her elbow and all but bundled her inside the room, leaving Molly to shut the door behind them. 'My brother, Lord Shalford, won't approve of our marriage and will do everything he can to put a stop to it. Better he don't know where we are until the knot's tied.'

'And my step-father, Sir John Radcliffe, would be of the same mind if he was to hear about it. I should like to know exactly why Lord Shalford is depriving you of your rightful income.'

'I'll explain everything whilst we eat. Look, I've ordered game-pie and fried potatoes, bread and cheese and apple pie and cream. There's buttermilk and lemonade for you and a decent claret for me.'

Not waiting for her to be seated he pulled out his chair and immediately tucked a napkin under his chin. Half smiling, Grace joined him at the table. He piled his plate leaving her to take what she wanted without his assistance. He might be charming but he appeared not to know the social niceties: that a gentleman must always seat a lady before himself and serve her first.

'I shall come into my inheritance on my marriage. Is it not the same for you?'

He nodded, pausing from his meal just long enough to answer. 'Indeed it is, Miss Hadley. My brother has taken against me and my friends and refuses to pay my bills. I can't abide being dunned by tailors and such. Bad form, you know, not to settle your bills on time.'

'I quite understand, Mr Shalford. There are one or two things we need to discuss before I agree.'

'Anything you like, I'm an easy-going sort of fellow.'

'I wish to live on your country estate in privacy. Do I have your word you will not bring down a house full of strange gentlemen?' He nodded and gestured with fork full of food that she continue. 'Also I wish it to be quite clear that my inheritance remains under my control.' She felt decidedly peculiar issuing orders in this way. Surely he must realise she had no right in law to dictate any such thing? She would only have his word that he would stick to the arrangement; once they were married he would have access to her trust fund and be able to do whatever he liked with it.

'I tell you what, Miss Hadley, you write all that down and then I'll sign it and have the landlord witness my signature. I have no wish to take your money, I just want to be able to be my own man and not under the control of my brother.'

'In which case, sir, I agree to marry you. I find I have no appetite; pray excuse me. I shall go at once and write

48

the necessary document. Will you be remaining here or retiring to your chamber?'

'Neither. Rolly Banister and Jack Simmons will be here any time and we're going to look at a racing curricle that's for sale in a village a mile or two away. Don't worry; I'll be back at five o'clock.' He drained his glass, refilling it for the fourth time.

Grace returned to her rooms with Molly trotting behind. 'Good job we still got the tray, miss, or you'd be going hungry this afternoon.'

* * *

The afternoon dragged by. Grace paced her sitting-room, becoming more agitated as five o'clock approached. She had changed her gown, washed and dried her hair and Molly had arranged this in a more becoming style. The paper stating her requirements had been written in duplicate and only awaited the signatures of both herself,

Mr Shalford and the witnesses.

'Molly, go down and see if Mr Shalford, the other two gentleman and the curate are waiting for us. I heard a church clock strike the hour; I have no wish to keep him waiting. The sooner this is over the happier I shall be.'

At half-past five the ceremony was over. A plain gold ring gleamed on her left hand. She had her copy of the statement safely in her reticule and the marriage certificate had been signed by the witnesses before the young curate had departed.

'Mr Shalford, I should prefer to dine in my room as you have your friends with you this evening. At what time are we to depart tomorrow morning?'

Her husband grinned. 'What a lark! Ralph will be mad as fire when he hears I'm married. You eat where you like, Miss Hadley . . . I beg your pardon, I should have said, Mrs Shalford. I shall remain here and get drunk with my friends.'

'Thank you. But you have not

answered my question about our departure, sir; what time do you wish me to be ready to leave in the morning?'

He shrugged. 'Best be off early, I sent a letter to my brother telling him I was getting married so it won't do to be around too long.'

Grace retreated to her rooms. She was puzzled why her husband had felt obliged to inform his brother of their marriage. She had no intention of telling her step-father, the more time that passed the better before he discovered her deception.

'It's a good thing we didn't send the tray back, madam, or you'd get no supper tonight,' Molly puffed from behind her.

'Indeed it is, Molly. I fear Mr Shalford is a young man too fond of his drink. I shall endeavour to keep away from him when he is in his cups.'

Around nine o'clock footsteps approached her parlour door. She clutched her book and prayed her new husband had not come to accost her. Molly opened the door and Mrs Turnbull curtsied.

'Mrs Shalford, I apologise for intruding, but I require your assistance.'

'How can I help?'

'It's like this, ma'am, Mr Shalford's gentlemen friends have left and he has passed out on the floor of the parlour. We don't like to leave him there, him being a gentleman and all.'

'I shall come at once. We must carry him to his bed chamber. My maid and I will take care of him. I am most grateful you have brought this to my attention.'

After a deal of struggling, two pot-boys and Mr Turnbull managed to transport the unconscious body of her husband to his bed chamber. Unfortunately they did not remain to help her disrobe him.

'I think we must just remove his neck cloth, his topcoat and boots, Molly, I would not feel comfortable doing more.'

'If we leave him on the side, put a chamber pot within his reach, I reckon he'll do. What could have possessed him to drink himself insensible?'

'He will be dead before he's thirty if he continues to abuse his body in this way. I think I shall sit up with him; I'd not want him to choke to death and become a widow on the same day I became a bride.'

The young man didn't stir during their ministrations. Molly propped him on his side by placing two pillows behind his back. He looked unwell, and far older than his years. 'He must be dreadfully unhappy, don't you think, Molly. He's a young man who has his whole life in front of him. Lord Shalford must indeed be a dreadful person to drive his brother into such a state.'

'Let me sit with him, madam, you go and get some rest.'

'Very well, but just for an hour. I shall take off my finery. Then you must sponge and press this outfit so it's ready for tomorrow.'

The desire to change was more to

protect her only smart ensemble from unpleasant consequences than to have her outfit cleaned. The church clock was striking eleven as she returned to the bedchamber. She sent Molly to her bed: there was no point in both of them being exhausted tomorrow.

She checked her patient was no worse and settled herself by the window. This was going to be a long night and the chamber was getting decidedly chilly. Restoring the fire would occupy her time and the flickering flames would be company. Never in her worst nightmares had she considered the first night of her marriage would be spent watching over a drunken stranger.

A Confrontation

Grace shifted on her chair; the padded seat seemed harder than when she'd sat down some hours ago. The fire was getting low; she shivered and pulled her shawl closer around her shoulders. A loud snore came from the bed at the far side of the room and her head jerked around.

Her husband showed no sign of waking. She relaxed and resumed her contemplation of the flames. As this was to be a marriage in name only should she be sitting in his room? She shuddered and her hands clenched in her lap, the new gold ring bit into her finger reminding her she'd taken her vows knowing full well they were meaningless.

A clock chimed. Thank goodness, it would be dawn soon and this miserable night would be over. A sudden commotion in the corridor outside the room alerted her. Surely her step-father could not have discovered her whereabouts so soon? She leapt to her feet and placed the bulk of the chair between herself and the door. Not a moment too soon; it slammed open and a huge, glowering gentleman filled the space.

He took in the situation at a glance and smiled grimly. 'I see I'm not too late to stop your tricks, madam. I'm Shalford, I'm here to remove my brother from your avaricious clutches.' The giant stepped in, closing the door in the curious face of the landlord.

He swayed and Grace saw his knuckles whiten where he gripped the mantel. Good grief, he was all but unconscious. What was it about these Shalford men that they were unable to stay on their feet like other people? Whilst she remained standing etiquette dictated he must not sit.

Hastily she sat, displaying her wedding ring prominently on the arm of the chair. She dare not raise her eyes to be fixed by his basilisk glare. This man was as terrifying and as formidable as Rupert had said. Small wonder he had been eager to marry in order to escape from his brother's tyranny. There was a thump as the intruder took the chair opposite hers, then nothing.

The chamber was strangely quiet. Why did he not continue to berate her? Nervously she raised her head to see her adversary as deeply asleep as his younger sibling. In repose he was less alarming, looked almost boyish, more like Rupert. She watched him for a few moments, allowing her breathing to return to normal.

Something quite extraordinary occurred to her. The man sprawled in the opposite chair, his caped greatcoat flowing around him, his boots caked with mud and his breeches just as bad, must have ridden the eighty miles from Shalford Hall. He had accomplished this feat in a few hours only. He could not possibly have received the letter from Rupert until late afternoon.

Despite his appalling rudeness she admired his achievement. He must be famished; his brother had not touched the supper tray brought up earlier. However unpleasant his lordship was, his temper might be improved by sustenance. She moved quietly to the table under the window where the meal had been left. Removing the napkin she examined the contents, she found it hard to distinguish the ham from the roast beef by the light of the single candle glimmering on the mantelshelf.

The bread was too hard to eat, but would do if she toasted it. The coffee was no more than lukewarm, but if she heated the poker and plunged it in it should be palatable. The apple pie and meat pasty would be as tasty cold as hot. First she must put coal and logs on the fire. She tiptoed back to the fireplace and knelt to remove what she needed from the log box and scuttle.

Ralph heard the woman move. He kept his limbs relaxed and peered through his lashes to see what she was about. She was out of sight and, without turning his head and alerting her he was awake, he couldn't see what she was doing. Perhaps a call of nature took her to the dressing-room.

No, she was beside him again. One by one she removed lumps of coal and placed them on the dying fire, this was followed by three small logs. He stiffened as she pushed the poker into the growing flames but did not remove it. God's teeth! Was she going to attack him whilst he slept?

She sat back on her heels and he saw her face clearly for the first time. He expected to see a painted jezebel — a light skirt his idiot brother had been inveigled into marrying. Instead he saw a young woman with nondescript dull brown hair worn in a severe, unflattering style, a pleasant countenance and brown eyes. Certainly nothing to suggest she was a femme fatale or a fortune hunter. In fact, she was a plain dab of a thing. She was as different from his expectations as chalk is to cheese.

There was something else going on here. Was it possible he'd jumped to the wrong conclusions? He watched her spring gracefully to her feet and move back across the room; she returned with a laden tray and placed it on a small foot stool in front of the fireplace. He tensed as she pulled out the poker but she plunged it into the coffee pot. Then she skewered two slices of bread on a toasting fork and held them in front of the flames.

His mouth began to water; he hadn't eaten since heaven knows when. His stomach rumbled loudly and the toast fell into the flames.

'Botheration! Now look what you've made me do.' Grace spoke without thinking, quite forgetting Shalford was her enemy.

A lean brown hand snaked past her and removed the bread before it was ruined. 'There, perfectly edible. Is that feast for me?'

'Rupert was unable to eat his supper. You might as well have it instead.' She stood up and moved away from the circle of light. For some reason she felt uncomfortable beneath his scrutiny. His strange tawny eyes fixed her like a hawk. 'Do not think I am going to wait on you, Shalford, I shall retire to my own chamber now that you're here to make sure Rupert doesn't choke.'

She hid her smile and headed for the door. With luck her comment would have put him off his supper. It had been a long night, perhaps now she would be able to sleep without fear. It had been too long since she'd had a peaceful night's slumber. Somehow she doubted her step-father would try and snatch her back when Lord Shalford was here.

She stumbled, stubbing her toe painfully on the doorstep. Good heavens! What nonsense was this? Rupert's autocratic brother had ridden pell-mell across country in order to prevent her marrying his brother. He would hand her back in a moment given half the chance. What had made her believe for an instant he would protect her?

Molly, was fast asleep on the truckle bed in the dressing-room. She would not disturb her; she was quite capable of removing her garments without assistance. Clad in her chemise she slipped between the covers, surprised that the sheets were not icy. Dearest Molly must have run the warming pan through them no more than an hour or so ago.

It scarcely seemed a quarter of an hour before she was roused by the sound of curtains rattling back on their poles. 'Molly, surely it's not time to get up already?'

'Bless you, madam, it's after eight o'clock. It has been that busy downstairs I had to queue to get your hot chocolate and warm water.' Molly bustled over, almost heaving Grace up the bed in her eagerness. 'Mr Shalford is waiting to speak to you, miss. I beg your pardon, madam. There have been two messages already asking when you will be going along to his chambers.'

'Lord Shalford arrived in the middle of the night, it will be he who's sending these demands. I'd best be quick, his lordship was not a man who will take kindly to being kept waiting.'

★　★　★

Ralph had no sympathy with his sibling's pounding headache or bilious attack. 'It serves you right, Rupert, I've warned you many times about drinking to excess. For heaven's sake drink your coffee and sit down, we have matters of the utmost importance to discuss.'

'Nothing you can say will make any difference. Grace and I were married in the sight of God and two witnesses. I am free of your interference, Ralph, I now have access to my inheritance and shall remove to my estate in Essex.' He pushed out his chin and glared, looking more like a spoilt schoolboy than a man old enough to have a wife. 'I am done with your rules and regulations, from now on I shall suit myself how I go on.'

'And whose idea was this folly?'

'Rolly Banister and Freddie said I couldn't do it, wagered one hundred guineas. Jack Simmons decided to help me.' He rubbed his forehead and sipped his coffee noisily.

'I see, I might have known those buffoons were involved. Where, if I might enquire, did you find Miss Hadley?'

'Jack's sister, I can't remember her name, was at school with her. She suggested Grace would be ideal as she was in a similar situation.' He scowled at Ralph. 'I'm twenty-one and can suit myself. If you're thinking she's not good enough, then you're wrong. Her grandpa was an earl or some such, her pa a colonel in the artillery. Mentioned in dispatches, I dare say.'

Ralph ground his teeth, barely restraining an impulse to tip a bucket of cold water over his brother. An unpleasant shock was exactly what the boy needed in order to come to his senses. 'I take it there is some reason why the young lady was prepared to tie herself to a fool like you? No doubt your money is enough to compensate for the lack of substance between your ears.'

'I say, that's a bit much.'

'I beg to differ. Only a complete ninny would marry for a wager — and to such a dull creature, too.' Ralph shook his head, quite baffled by Rupert's inability to see what was obvious. He would have to make it clear. 'No woman of sense would contract herself to a complete stranger unless there was a pressing need to do so. She must be with child and intending to foist her child off on you.' His brother's shocked expression did nothing to reassure him.

'Grace married me to get away from her step-father. Sir John Radcliffe has been using the interest from her inheritance to fund his gambling. Not satisfied with this, he was going to coerce her into marrying one of his friends and then split the trust fund with her husband. I'll not have you say such things about her.'

For the second time Ralph wondered if he'd misjudged his putative sister-in-law. Perhaps her reasons for embarking on this unsuitable arrangement were not avaricious after all. He would make enquiries, someone would know if the girl was indeed an heiress, or a fortune hunter as he suspected.

'Whoever she is, she is taking a devil of a long time to appear.' He frowned as he viewed his brother's dishevelment. 'I suggest you go back into your bed chamber and let Evans improve your appearance. It's a good thing he arrived this morning with your carriage. I'll not have you letting down the family by greeting Miss Hadley in clothes you've slept in.' Ralph's lips quirked, at least one Shalford would be clean and respectable. His togs had yet to appear; they were travelling behind him in his coach. Evans had done his best to improve matters but he was still decidedly unkempt, not something he was accustomed to.

Rupert waved a limp hand but remained slumped in the armchair. 'I'm not well enough to bother about such niceties. Grace won't mind how I look. She's a game girl, a crumpled shirt don't offend her.'

★　★　★

Grace paused outside the parlour door, waiting for her pulse to steady. The thought of being interrogated by that arrogant, objectionable man was not a pleasant one. Nevertheless, it must be done. She drew herself up, straightened her shoulders and pinned on a polite smile. As she was raising her hand to knock she heard Lord Shalford speaking.

'Get up. Do it now. I don't give a damn what Miss Hadley thinks, it is I that am offended by your indolence.'

She froze, uncertain whether to proceed or retreat to the safety of her own apartment. Then anger replaced her fear. Rupert was her responsibility now. How dare that horrid man speak to her husband in that way? She pushed open the door with rather more vigour than she intended and it crashed back with as much noise as Shalford had produced when he'd appeared so unexpectedly.

Two heads shot round. Rupert grinned, apparently unbothered by his older brother's rudeness. However, Shalford's lips thinned and his tiger eyes flashed dangerously.

'Good morning, Rupert, I'm relieved to see you up and about. I expect you have a headache this morning.' Grace ignored the fuming man towering above her and walked over to join her husband. 'I expect you would rather postpone our departure until tomorrow, my dear. I am perfectly content to stay another day.' She gestured towards the windows. 'Indeed, it is most inclement today, not at all seasonable for April. Much better to remain in front of a warm fire.'

She could almost hear Shalford's teeth grinding. Treating him as discourteously as he had treated her was most enjoyable. Then Rupert's expression changed to one of alarm. Too late. She turned and he loomed over her.

'Enough of this nonsense, madam. Do you think I intend to stand here listening to you two simpletons discuss the weather?'

It would have been better to have remained silent but something prompted Grace to tip back her head and stare directly at him. 'I have no idea of your intentions, my lord, I am not a clairvoyant after all.' If he had been furious before, now he was incandescent. She saw his hands clench, bright spots of colour appeared along his cheekbones and instinctively she stepped backwards.

In her haste her heel caught on the hem of her gown. She teetered, then lost her balance. The same strong hands reached out just before her head cracked against the mantelshelf. Heart pounding, she was lifted to safety. She rested her cheek against his chest for a second, could hear a corresponding thumping beneath her ear. Then she was dumped unceremoniously on a chaise-longue and his lordship was once more towering above her, his face hard and uncompromising.

Rupert finally reacted. 'My word, that was a close call. If Ralph hadn't caught you . . . '

'In which case it's fortunate I did so. Whilst you are changing your apparel, Miss Hadley and I can begin our discussion.'

Grace was too shaken to protest at his high-handed behaviour and his incorrect usage of her former name; Rupert pushed himself unsteadily upright and tottered off to his bed chamber.

Despite her upset, her mood lightened. She'd only known him a short while, but she was quite sure it would be at least an hour before he returned. Unfortunately he favoured the macaroni school of fashion, luridly striped waistcoats and shirt points so high he was unable to turn his head with any degree of comfort.

She risked a glance at Shalford. He was preoccupied, frowning after his brother and she was able to stare freely. Without his riding coat and dressed in the best that Weston could produce, she was forced to admit he made a fine figure of a man. At almost a head taller than Rupert, and much broader in the chest, he filled his dark blue, superfine jacket to perfection. His hair was not the colour of ripe corn, like Rupert's, more honey coloured.

'Do I meet with your approval, Miss Hadley?'

Her eyes flew down to meet his amused gaze. She felt the heat spreading from her toes to her crown. Drat the man for making her uncomfortable yet again. 'Your exterior is quite satisfactory, not the equal to Rupert's of course, but good enough, I suppose.' There was a flash of something that could have been admiration reflected in his eyes. Emboldened she continued. 'However, one must not judge a book by its cover, must one, my lord?' There was no need for her to elaborate, she'd made her meaning abundantly clear.

Instead of reacting angrily, his mouth widened in a smile that made her toes curl in their slippers. 'Well said, my dear girl. Now, preliminary skirmishes over, can we talk about what really matters?' He stretched out and picked up a heavy oak chair, lifted it as if it weighed nothing at all, and folded his long length on to it.

'I have no wish to discuss anything without my husband being present, my lord. I'm sure you understand. It's not my place . . . '

'Fustian! We both know Rupert will be incapable of saying anything sensible until tomorrow.' He leant forward, pinning her like a butterfly to a board with his fierce stare.

'Why did you marry my brother? If you have your own fortune, then you were not motivated by greed.' He allowed her no time to reply then continued, his expression grim. 'There can be only one explanation, you are expecting a child . . . '

Grace surged to her feet, closed the gap between them and dealt him a resounding slap. The crack of the blow echoed around the room. 'How dare you suggest such a thing? You are despicable; I never wish to see you again. You are *persona non grata* in your brother's life from this moment on.'

The Truth Is Spoken

Grace tumbled into her chamber and lent against the door expecting at any moment his lordship would arrive and demand entry. She pressed her ear to the wood but could hear no sign of pursuit.

'Lawks, madam, whatever next? You're as white as a sheet. Come along and sit yourself down.' Molly tutted and muttered under her breath as she escorted Grace to a convenient armchair.

'Is there a lock on the door, Molly? Quickly push it across. I struck Lord Shalford and he might be on his way to extract restitution.' Her maid moved with remarkable speed for a plump lady in her middle years and Grace felt the tension in her chest slowly dissipate as the bolt was rammed home. She was safe, at least for the moment.

Her left hand smarted; what could

have possessed her to behave in such an unladylike way? For the past few years she had bitten her tongue and held back her anger at the unkind treatment she had received at the hands of her step-father. Yet she had just struck a complete stranger with less provocation than she'd had many times before.

This was a conundrum, and not one she was prepared to consider at the moment. How dare he suggest she was not an innocent young lady? Righteous indignation flooded through her again and when there was a brisk knock at the door, instead of cowering back in her chair, she jumped to her feet and called for Molly.

'There's someone at the door. Please come and see who it is.'

Her abigail pulled back the bolt and opened the door a fraction. Instead of it being shoved rudely open a respectful voice enquired. 'I would like to speak to Miss Hadley.'

Molly closed the door in Shalford's face. 'Shall I let him in, madam?'

With a sigh of resignation Grace nodded. 'Yes, please do so. However, I wish you to remain in the room.'

He strolled in as if nothing untoward had taken place, as if a scarlet handprint was not glowing on his right cheek. He stared pointedly at Molly, but her maid moved to stand behind Grace's chair ignoring his unspoken command.

'I have no wish to speak to you, Lord Shalford. However I am prepared to listen to your apology for Rupert's sake, but then you will leave.'

His eyes widened and for a moment he looked quite disconcerted. Then he recovered his aplomb and almost bowed. 'I wish to speak to you in private, ma'am. Until your servant has removed herself I shall remain silent.'

Grace turned. 'Please go, Molly, I'm sure there are plenty of tasks for you to do elsewhere.'

Shalford had wandered to the window and turned his back, but she could see his shoulders were rigid, he was not as relaxed as he wished to appear. She had a moment's misgiving as Molly closed the parlour door, leaving her alone with this irascible aristocrat. He swung round and she swallowed the lump in her throat as his fingers casually traced the imprint of her hand.

'May I be seated?' His tone was bland, his expression watchful. She shrugged and gestured towards an upright chair. She didn't trust her voice so ventured no reply. He continued in the same even measure, as if he was discussing the weather. 'No-one has ever struck me. They would not be so foolhardy. Yet you, a mouse of a woman, has done so.' He leant forward. 'What do you suggest I do about it?'

This was a ludicrous question and restored her equanimity. 'You deserved it. I am still waiting to hear your apology.' She glared at him, daring him to contradict. Her words caused him to surge out of his chair and for a terrifying moment she thought he would grip her arms and drag her upright.

He stood no more than a yard from her, his face like granite. 'I apologise? Have you run mad, woman? It is you who should be on your knees begging my forgiveness.'

Something prompted her to jump out of her chair and confront him. 'I did not accuse you of being impure. If I had a brother he would be entitled to run you through for such an insult. I believe that you got off lightly in the circumstances.'

For a moment it hung in the balance, his hands were clenched at his sides, a pulse hammered at the base of his neck. She stood her ground, he would not hurt her physically, he might strip her to the bone with the lash of his tongue but instinctively she knew he would never raise his hand.

'Good grief! You are an original and quite correct to castigate me.' This time he bowed deeply as if meeting her for the first time. 'I apologise profoundly for my appalling accusation. I hope you will accept it and we can start again.'

When he straightened she responded with a similar curtsy. 'And I apologise for striking you. Please be seated, my lord, I believe we have much to talk about.' As she spoke she realised the absurdity of her words, she should be speaking to her husband, not to his older brother.

This time he didn't move the chair any closer. 'I understand that you became involved in this . . . this unfortunate venture because you wish to be away from Sir John Radcliffe. Do you know why my idiot brother married you?'

'Rupert told me he was in a similar position to me, had reached his majority but was unable to run his own life without interference.' She hesitated, not sure she could continue in this vein, but the matter must be clear between them. 'He said you were a trifle autocratic and demanding. By marrying he would be able to access his inheritance and live as he pleased.' Why was he staring at her as if she were a candidate for Bedlam? 'Having experienced your high-handed behaviour for myself, sir, I have every sympathy with his desire to be free of your influence.'

'God in his heaven! I have no wish to disillusion you, my dear, but contrary to your belief I am a perfectly reasonable fellow and only interfere with Rupert's life by paying off his gambling debts and . . . ' his cheeks coloured and he ran his finger around his neck cloth as if it had grown too tight for some reason 'and extricating him from unwise liaisons.' He sat back in his chair and smiled sadly. 'It is true recently I gave him an ultimatum. Unless he mended his ways he would have to live on his allowance. I'm afraid I must be blunt, Rupert married you for a wager.'

'I don't believe it. Why are you telling me such tales? I've only known your brother a few hours, but one thing I am certain of he is not an unkind gentleman. He would not lie to me, deceive me . . . ' Her voice faltered beneath his sympathetic gaze.

'I can't tell you how sorry I am, my dear, but I can assure you, Rupert married you for the princely sum of one hundred guineas. Of course, he might also have been prompted by the reasons he gave you, but he can never resist a wager. Something you could not possibly know after such a short acquaintance is that he is already a hardened gambler, will wager on the length of time it takes a raindrop to trickle down a pane of glass given the opportunity.'

Unwanted tears prickled behind her eyelids. She blinked them back, swallowed hard and came to a decision. 'In which case, my lord, I wish the marriage to be terminated as speedily as possible. I believe that if a couple have not consummated the union . . . ' Her face turned an unbecoming shade of beetroot and his eyebrows shot beneath his hair.

'Exactly so. I am not without

influence in Parliament and can expedite this matter; you must return to Shalford Hall with me and I shall set things in motion.'

Thoroughly discomfited by the turn the conversation had taken, Grace scrambled to her feet with more speed than elegance. 'I have no intention of going anywhere with you. An old school friend has invited me to make my home with her, she is about to be confined with her second child and does not have the wherewithal to employ a suitable companion. I shall arrange a passage for myself on the next mail coach; you have no need to be concerned on my behalf.'

He loomed over her, she barely restrained her impulse to step back. 'My carriage will be here very soon, allow me to put it at your disposal. You would not be in this predicament but for my sibling's disgraceful behaviour. It is the least I can do.'

His offer was made so handsomely it would seem churlish to refuse. 'In which case, I thank you. My friend, Mrs Cunningham, resides in a small village on the other side of Romford. I fear your vehicle will not be returned to you for several days.'

'I will hear no more of this nonsense, Miss Hadley, if you would care to write down the exact direction I shall have one of my outriders go ahead to book your accommodation. I take it you have no wish to speak to Rupert before you leave?'

'Certainly not. I should never have agreed to this arrangement if I had known the true circumstances. However dire my own situation I would not have been wed for a wager.' She stared pointedly at the door and he took the hint. He bowed and, with a polite smile, strolled out.

'Well I never! Who would have thought Mr Shalford could treat you so shabbily, miss. You are well rid of him, and it won't be so bad with Mrs Cunningham.'

'It will be intolerable. Isobel will

expect me to wait on her hand and foot and no doubt you will become a member of her household staff as well. We must both grit our teeth and get on with it, anything is preferable to remaining under the control of Sir John. I'm sure that four years will soon pass.' Even as she spoke she knew she was not fooling herself or her maid. But she had no alternative, this sham marriage was no longer an acceptable alternative.

'I'll get on with packing your trunk, Miss Hadley. It is ever so kind of his lordship to let you use his travelling carriage, so much nicer than going by the common stage.'

'Indeed it is, Molly. We must make the most of such luxuries for I doubt we will have access to any sort of carriage for the foreseeable future. Can you go down and cancel our seats for tomorrow and claim the refund?'

Ralph thought he had handled the situation far better than he had anticipated. He had controlled his temper, apologised handsomely and secured the result he'd ridden eighty miles to achieve. He hummed a tune to himself as he strode through the busy coaching inn and out into the yard to greet his coachman.

Having issued his instructions he went round to the stable block to check that his stallion, Caliban, had recovered from his exertions the previous day. The groom who'd accompanied him on a massive bay gelding, greeted him politely.

'Both horses are fighting fit, my lord. They'll be ready to go this afternoon.'

'Excellent, there's no need for us to return at such a dangerous pace. Digby has taken my portmanteau to my chamber, I intend to spruce myself up, partake of a substantial luncheon and then set off. We shall overnight this time, I've sent Sam Tufnell to reserve accommodation.'

His business accomplished outside he returned to his chamber for a leisurely wash and shave, knowing that in the competent hands of Digby he would be returned to his usual sartorial elegance.

★　★　★

Grace could only pick at her luncheon tray; she was too upset about Rupert's perfidy. Molly informed her the carriage in which they were to travel to Essex was the height of luxury, a great improvement on the journey they had taken when she had fled from her ancestral home. It grieved her to think Sir John was now left to occupy the mansion which had been in the possession of the Hadleys for countless generations. There being no male to inherit the title, it had fallen into abeyance on her grandfather's death. However, the property and fortune had descended to her mother.

She shook her head; high time she put these things behind her. Sir John had wormed his way into her mother's affections and married her not two years after dear Papa had passed away.

Thank God Grandpa had shown the foresight to protect the estates from this man's depredations. Sir John could not touch the capital or take money from the estates, but had free access to the interest and had somehow persuaded the lawyers he should be a trustee for her own inheritance.

The only way she could prevent him from spending this was by absenting herself from Hadley Manor. She had already sent a letter to the legal firm in London, which dealt with the family's affairs, informing them that she no longer resided with Sir John and therefore he had no reason to demand funds on her behalf.

Two burly grooms arrived to transport her trunk and other bags to the waiting vehicle. She could delay her departure no longer; there was still a risk that Sir John had somehow discovered she was not intending to return. No, she had given him an incorrect address — even if he came to look for her when she failed to reappear he would not find her easily.

She looked round as she was handed into the carriage half expecting either Rupert or his formidable brother to appear to bid her farewell. However, neither of them came out and she wasn't sure if she was disappointed or relieved. She had slept little the previous night so asked Molly to pull down the blinds. Warm rugs, soft pillows and hot bricks had been provided for their comfort and she settled down to rest. The day was overcast and cold and the extra comforts were welcome.

She was woken when the carriage rocked to a standstill. Flustered she sat up to see Molly fast asleep in the corner. 'Quickly, Molly, we have stopped. Please make sure my bonnet is not awry.'

She had barely completed the repair to her appearance when the door opened and the steps were let down. The night was dark, lanterns swung crazily in the gusty wind and she hurried inside the building not looking to left or right. They were immediately conducted to a superior bedchamber with both dressing-room and parlour.

'I am fair starved, Miss Hadley, I do hope they keep a good table here. There's a fine bed for me in the dressing-room, I'll not have to use a truckle tonight.' Molly busied herself unpacking the necessary night things, leaving Grace to stroll around the substantial sitting-room.

Scarcely five minutes passed before two chambermaids staggered in bearing trays laden with every sort of delicacy. These were placed on a convenient table then crisp white napery was spread on a second table and a chair placed ready for Grace to sit. 'Good heavens, all this cannot be for me?'

'We had instructions to provide you with the best supper The Green Man can provide. Cook has sent a portion of everything on the menu tonight.' The girl bobbed. 'Would you be wishing us to stay and serve you, miss?'

'No, thank you, my maid will do that. However, I should like hot water sent in an hour.'

'We'll be bringing up your bath water directly, miss. It'll be piping hot, just right for when you're ready.'

Such luxury! She began to feel more kindly disposed towards Shalford for he had made her journey as comfortable as possible. Her appetite had returned and was able to do justice to the repast. Molly assisted her into the bath in the dressing-room and then returned to eat her own supper from what remained.

The next morning she was served piping hot chocolate and sweet morning rolls at half-past six, at seven she was once again safely installed in Lord Shalford's luxurious travelling carriage. As she had never travelled to Essex before there were no landmarks for her to look out for. However, in her estimation she should arrive at the village of Ingatestone by lunchtime at the latest.

Isobel had informed her the area in

which she lived was not far from the toll road, so it seemed strange that they were travelling in the depths of the country. Why were they obliged to stop for luncheon and then continue their journey? 'Coachman, when should we reach Ingatestone? I had no idea the journey was going to take so long.'

'We'll be at our destination before dark. Remember, miss, these beasts have already travelled a fair distance these past few days. Wouldn't do to exhaust them.'

'Of course not, how stupid of me, I did not consider this could be the reason we were taking so long to arrive.'

Dusk had fallen when the carriage slowed and then turned sharply. The blinds were once more down; by the time Molly had scrambled up and peered round she was too late to see why they had veered right in that fashion. 'It's mighty strange, miss, but I reckon we're travelling down somebody's drive. This don't look like no country lane I've ever been in.'

Grace shot up, her fatigue forgotten. Surely not? He could not have done something so underhand. 'Roll up the blinds, open the window, I wish to see where we're going.' She hung out of the window like an urchin and was not overly surprised to see an enormous edifice, hundreds of windows glittering with candlelight and a small army of liveried retainers gathered on the gravel turning circle waiting for them.

Lord Shalford had royally tricked her. She was at Shalford Hall; there could be no other explanation.

A Companion

'I am so looking forward to meeting Miss Hadley, she must be an exceptional young lady to have made such an impact on both my sons.'

'Mama, I must warn you she is of uncertain temper and indifferent appearance.' Ralph smiled as he saw the carriage turn into the long drive. 'At last, she will be here in a few minutes. By the way, do not expect Miss Hadley to be overjoyed at being here.'

'Whatever do you mean? Why should she not be delighted to be invited to Shalford Hall?' His mother attempted to push herself out of her chair and he rushed to her side to assist.

'Unfortunately the young lady refused my invitation and I was obliged to use subterfuge in order to get her here.' Gently he slipped his arm around her waist and lifted her to her feet. He guided her to the window. 'Look, our unwilling guest has just realised my deception.' Miss Hadley had just appeared at the window of the carriage.

'Ralph, you're incorrigible. Where exactly did the poor girl think she was going?'

'To some benighted village the other side of Romford in order to live with a friend as an unpaid servant. Miss Hadley is a lady and I cannot allow her to spend the next few years being mistreated.' He glanced down at his mother and saw she was smiling in a most particular way.

'I see; whatever the reasons are for her visit, it will be a treat for me to have intelligent female company. I am disposed to like her already.' Lady Shalford reached up and brushed his injured cheek. 'However, dearest, I am at a loss to understand why you should be taking such an interest in her.'

He frowned, he had no sensible answer to that question. 'Her predicament has become my concern as

Rupert's stupidity caused her to contract a meaningless marriage. It is my intention to have it annulled as soon as possible, for all our sakes, and it will be far easier to do this if Miss Hadley is residing here and can sign the legal papers and do whatever else is necessary.'

'Then I shall make every effort to welcome her and apologise for your high-handed behaviour. She has every right to be incensed for being tricked in this way, I pray I can persuade her to remain here.'

'She will have no choice. It is more than ten miles to the nearest coaching inn, I doubt even someone as determined as Miss Hadley would attempt to walk that distance.' He grinned at his mother's outraged expression. 'Pray, Mama, do not poker up at me. I had no option. I am relying on you to smooth matters over for me. I shall absent myself, I have no wish to be on the receiving end of another slap, however much I might deserve one.' He could hear his mother laughing as he retreated.

The carriage rocked to a standstill and immediately was surrounded by attentive footmen. Grace was escorted from the vehicle as if she was an honoured guest and not an unwelcome visitor. She expected to be greeted by his lordship, but his housekeeper and butler bowed and curtsied to her when she reached the impressive front door.

'Miss Hadley, welcome to Shalford Hall. Lady Shalford is waiting to greet you in her apartment.' The butler almost smiled. 'I am Foster, at your service.'

'I should like to refresh myself before I meet her ladyship.'

'Certainly, Miss Hadley. The house-keeper, Brown, will conduct you to your apartment herself. I hope your stay here will be enjoyable. Anything you want, please ask.'

Grace followed the tall, spare woman dressed in grey, up the handsome oak staircase, much impressed by what she

to greet you. As you can see I am somewhat infirm. Come in, I have sent for refreshments as I expect you are sharp set after your long journey, and it is an age until dinnertime.' Grace hurried forward and dropped on to the upright chair beside her ladyship. 'Also, there's no need to pretend you are glad to be here. My reprehensible son has told me how he tricked you into coming.'

Grace liked this delightful lady already, she was quite different from either of her children. 'Actually, and I beg you not to tell Shalford this, I would much prefer to be here in such luxury and comfort than with my friend in Romford taking care of her children.'

Lady Shalford reached out and clasped her hands. 'I knew it, when Ralph told me what he'd done I was sure there was something special about you.' She smiled sweetly. 'Much as I love him, I am the first to admit he is not the most sociable of creatures. To have invited a complete stranger to live with us is quite unprecedented.' She paused as two parlour maids glided in and placed a delicious array of cakes, scones and patties on a side table and the tea urn and other paraphernalia on another.

'Would you like me to make the tea, my lady?' Grace would much prefer to do it rather than have the servants hovering in the background.

'Thank you, my dear, that would be so kind. I prefer mine without milk or sugar.'

Twenty minutes later Grace sat back, dabbing her lips on a damask napkin. 'That was quite delicious, I hadn't realised just how hungry I was. I do hope dinner is not be served until midnight, I could not eat another morsel.'

'Ralph must dine on his own tonight. Neither of us will require further sustenance after that feast.' Lady Shalford picked up a small brass bell and rang it vigorously. Instantly the same two girls whisked in and removed the debris. Once they were alone her hostess pursed her lips. 'My dear, forgive me, but would you mind standing up and walking back and forth across the carpet?'

Surprised, but willing, Grace did as she was asked. 'Would you like me to practice my curtsy whilst I'm up?'

Laughing Lady Shalford waved her back into her seat. 'No, child, but I should like you to move your chair closer, if you wouldn't mind?'

This accomplished Grace waited expectantly, intrigued by these peculiar requests. To her astonishment a delicate hand reached out and lifted a strand of hair. Her ladyship rubbed it between her fingers before sitting back.

'Exactly as I thought. Tell me, child, why do you dye your hair with walnut juice and wear such unflattering garments? From whom are you hiding?' The direct gaze, so startlingly like Shalford's but the colour of Rupert's, demanded an honest reply.

'When my mother . . . when Mama

was dying she told me to make myself invisible. That way my step-father might well forget I was there and not attempt to involve me in his nefarious schemes and unpleasant house parties.'

'Well, you have no need to remain unnoticed here.' She clapped her hands. 'You are exactly what I need to get me back on my feet again. You shall assist me and I shall restore you to your natural beauty.' Her delightful tinkling laugh filled the room. 'What a surprise my boys will have when they find their mama walking again and that the apparently plain Miss Hadley is a lovely young woman.'

'I fear one part of your plan is doomed to failure, ma'am. I am no beauty, you will be disappointed on that score.'

'Nonsense, my dear, under that hideous garment you have a beautiful figure. You carry yourself well and when your hair is restored to its natural colour and you are dressed in fashionable gowns you will not know yourself.'

Grace had to stop this fairy tale. 'I'm afraid that I do not have the wherewithal to purchase a new wardrobe. Sir John has control of my fortune.'

Lady Shalford beamed. 'I told you, my dear, you are to be my project; therefore any expense shall be mine. Just think how Ralph and Rupert will react when they see us both restored?'

Now was not the time to remind her ladyship that she doubted either of the Shalford men would be in the slightest bit interested in her, however she was dressed. However, Grace was more than ready to help Lady Shalford recover her mobility. 'I have thought of a slight snag, my lady. It will be easy to surprise Rupert, for he is not here to see the transformation. Will not Lord Shalford notice as my hair slowly changes colour?'

'I have thought of that. You must move into my chambers, I have a delightful guest room. We shall tell Ralph you are to remain here as my companion and are therefore no further

105

concern of his.' The bell was rung again and this time Foster appeared. 'Foster, have Brown arrange for the transfer of Miss Hadley's belongings here. Also inform Lord Shalford that in future we shall dine together in my sitting-room.'

The august gentleman bowed. 'Certainly, my lady. I shall have it done at once.'

'There, my dear, the matter is settled. I cannot tell you how excited I am. I know we have only just met, but it is as if we have been acquainted for ever.' She raised a finely arched eyebrow. 'How long is it before you have control of your fortune?'

'There is a further three years to wait . . . '

'Then you must remain here under my protection until then. No, I will brook no protests. Consider this your home. We shall have such fun together, there's nothing I like better than tormenting Ralph and together we shall shake him out of his complacency.'

Things were happening too fast.

Much as she liked Lady Shalford she was quite as high-handed as her oldest son, although in a far less autocratic manner. From whichever way one viewed it, they both were interfering with her life. It would not do, she had left one impossible situation to find herself in another. A gilded cage was still a cage, after all.

Hiding her dismay at having her life rearranged without her permission, Grace smiled. 'It's most gracious of you, my lady, but you must not go to any expense on my account. However, whilst I am residing here I shall be more than happy to become involved in your rehabilitation.'

* * *

Ralph listened with incredulity as his butler informed him solemnly that Miss Hadley, in the space of one half hour, had somehow metamorphosed from a temporary and unwanted guest into the bosom bow of his mother. 'I see. Lady

Shalford has moved Miss Hadley into her rooms? I am to dine alone in future?'

Foster shifted from one foot to the other. 'That is correct, my lord.'

'Very well. In which case there's no need to go to all the bother of preparing the dining-room in future. I also will dine in my apartment until Lady Shalford decrees otherwise.'

He felt an almost irresistible urge to throw the book at the door as it closed behind his servant. Miss Hadley had turned his well-ordered life into chaos. The wretched woman had somehow entwined herself into all their lives. Firstly she had married his brother and secondly she had persuaded his mama to make her a permanent resident here. But far more important, her interference would now condemn him to eat a lonely dinner every night.

It would not do. Miss Hadley had taken on an opponent she could not best. He would not be manipulated in his own home. He straightened and carefully replaced the book on the shelf. He wasn't a gambling man, the trait had passed him by, thank God. What he liked was the challenge of defeating an adversary, whether it be in business, sport or anything else.

Miss Hadley would be gone from Shalford the moment the marriage was dissolved. She might believe she was settled, could stay at his expense for the next three years, but she was in for an unpleasant surprise. She would get her comeuppance soon enough; he couldn't wait.

⋆ ⋆ ⋆

Over the next two weeks Grace frequently spotted Lord Shalford in the grounds, but was always able to dodge behind a statue or tree and avoid being seen. His mother's plans were working well; the walnut juice had almost gone after frequently washing her hair in camomile water. Lady Shalford was making a determined effort to walk without assistance, she was still decidedly unsteady but the improvement was all but miraculous.

'My dear Grace, I do believe that all I needed was a reason to get out of my chair. I have been decidedly melancholy these past few months.'

'Indeed, ma'am, I was feeling much the same. We are a tonic to each other.' She nodded towards the buttercup silk gown draped over the back of a chair. 'I cannot wait to wear that dress. I haven't worn anything colourful since my mother passed away three years ago.'

'Then it's high time you started making the most of yourself. I can't wait to see Ralph's face when we walk in to the grand salon tomorrow night.'

Grace shook her head. 'Do you think you should attempt the stairs so soon, my lady? Although you are walking more smoothly around your apartment, we have not yet attempted stairs.'

'Fiddlesticks to that! When Ralph came to see me this morning he told me he was dining out tonight. I shall practise whilst he is away.' She chuckled at Grace's horrified expression. 'Please, don't worry; I shall make sure I have two stout footmen on hand in case I need assistance.'

'Good heavens, that's Rupert's phaeton turning into the drive. I would know those dashing chestnuts anywhere.'

Immediately Lady Shalford joined her at the window. 'You are quite correct. No doubt he will come immediately to see his mama, you must hide yourself away. Quickly, dear girl, take your gown and slippers.' She clapped her hands like a small child. 'How exciting, now we can astonish both of them at the same time.'

Grace smiled fondly at the lady who had already become a dear friend. Despite the discrepancy in their ages, she treated Lady Shalford as a contemporary, not the mother of the formidable Lord Shalford. 'The only problem is that now we cannot practise the stairs.'

'I shall send Rupert out with his brother, he will not quibble.' For a moment her ladyship looked as indomitable as her eldest son. It would seem that not only did the two men get their startling good looks and corn-coloured hair from their maternal parent, they also got her fierceness of spirit.

'I shall make myself scarce.' Grace moved rapidly to the exit, where she paused. 'I still have several other ensembles to try on. I can hardly credit the mantua maker and her team of seamstresses managed to complete so much in such a short space of time.'

Lady Shalford waved an airy hand. 'Anything can be achieved if you give the right incentive.'

Oh dear! This must mean that the cost of the new wardrobe had been exorbitant. Grace was about to suggest that when she came into her inheritance she reimbursed the sum when her ladyship spoke again.

'I told Madame Ducray she would do well to achieve the impossible, as you

112

are likely to be the future Lady Shalford.'

Grace dropped the precious gown. Her hands flew to her cheeks, they were burning beneath her fingertips. 'How could you say such a thing? His lordship will be so angry. I would rather dress in rags than have had you . . . '

'Do not look so distressed, dearest girl. I have sworn Madame to secrecy on pain of losing my custom. I would not have dreamt of saying anything so compromising if I had had the slightest suspicion the information would become common knowledge.'

'I pray that is the case, my lady. I believe my tenure here shall come to an abrupt end if such a falsehood comes to Shalford's ears. It beggars belief that I appear to be married to one of your sons and betrothed to another.'

Not wishing to discuss the matter further, Grace fled to the comparative privacy of her own bedchamber. All desire to try on her new clothes deserted her, she prowled around her domain, her thoughts in turmoil. The sooner the lawyers completed the necessary papers and she could remove herself from this place the better. The longer she was here the more entangled she became in a web of deceit.

What was it about this family that made them behave so irrationally? Then the absurdity of the situation struck her. If she had not agreed to this ridiculous marriage then Rupert would not have behaved deceitfully, would no doubt have moved on to some other ridiculous wager. Shalford would not have accused her of being a lady of doubtful morals and his mother would not have told the dressmaker that Grace and Shalford were betrothed.

From whichever way she viewed things, she could come to no other conclusion, that her own foolishness had led to this unfortunate state of affairs. An irresistible urge to giggle welled up inside her, his lordship must be as cross as she about things. On the positive side, however, Lady Shalford had recovered her *joie de vivre* and whatever the outcome between the two Shalford men and herself their mother would be left in a better position both emotionally and physically.

She settled herself comfortably in front of the apple-log fire, tucked her stockinged feet beneath her skirt and picked up the most delightful book she had discovered on the bookshelf in her parlour. The book was entitled 'Pride & Prejudice' and she could not remember having enjoyed a novel as much as this one.

From her rooms she couldn't hear what transpired between Rupert and his mama, but she saw Shalford and his brother leave in a closed carriage at dusk. This was the opportune moment to return to Lady Shalford and the attempt on the stairs. She was greeted as if she had been missing for months and not merely in her room for a few hours.

'Dearest girl, such fun! I cannot wait to tell you the extraordinary reason

Rupert has given for appearing here today. I don't expect to see him apart from the festive season, on my birthday and when he is recovering. He remains in town with his cronies.'

'I believe, my lady, that he is obliged to sign the same papers that I am in order to dissolve our marriage.'

'There you have it. He does not wish to dissolve the marriage, he has decided that he is in love with you and wishes to persuade you to make this a genuine contract.'

Grace sank into the nearest chair, quite unable to make a rational comment to this extraordinary announcement. Her hostess waited patiently. 'I am stunned, my lady. Rupert has no more wish to be married than I — what nonsense has got into his brain this time?'

'Of course he doesn't have genuine feelings for you, it is infatuation merely. However, it will be amusing watching him attempt to interest you and Ralph doing his best to keep you apart.'

'Forgive me for speaking bluntly, Lady Shalford, but it will be anything but amusing for me. I have no wish to be a bone of contention between your sons. I must make it quite clear, as soon as this wretched business is sorted I shall be leaving here.'

Lady Shalford seemed unbothered by this frank statement; she raised an eyebrow and nodded as if agreeing. 'Let's say no more about it, you must do whatever you wish, my dear. This is not a prison, when you are ready to leave you may do so whatever Ralph or Rupert think of the matter.' She slipped her arm through hers and smiled. 'Come along, I must brave the stairs. Have you not noticed how agile I'm becoming.'

'Indeed, my lady, you are walking quite normally now. I take it that you remained in your chair whilst Rupert was visiting?'

'Yes, I made a great play of having him fetch me things as if I was deteriorating rather than improving.'

In the spacious passageway the housekeeper, butler and two footmen were waiting expectantly. They had all been sworn to silence. No word of this miracle was to reach the ears of the Shalford men until the dramatic appearance of their mother tomorrow night.

'If you were to hold on to the banister, my lady, I can walk beside you. The footmen must descend the stairs backwards, one step in front of us. That way if you were to fall they would be ready to catch you.'

For all her bravado Grace sensed Lady Shalford was fearful of taking the first step. It had been several months since she had left her apartment, it must be daunting facing a wide staircase with so many stairs.

As it happened the matter was accomplished with more ease than either of them had expected. Less than half an hour later Grace was back in her ladyship's apartment sitting down to a delicious repast.

'The food would be so much more tasty, my lady, if it arrived here piping hot. No doubt in this vast establishment your kitchens are half a mile away.'

'I believe that is a slight exaggeration, my love, but I agree it's high time Ralph modernised below stairs. At my insistence he installed bathing rooms, but as far as I am aware the kitchens remain as they have always been.' She smiled archly. 'Perhaps you might suggest the improvements?'

Laughing at the ridiculous suggestion, Grace picked up her heavy silver cutlery. Despite its lack of warmth the fricassee of hare, boiled rice and buttered carrots was excellent. The waiting chambermaids cleared the table and produced a charlotte russe for dessert.

'Shall we play a hand or two of Piquet or do you wish to return to that novel you are so engrossed in?'

'I should be delighted to play cards with you, madam, but I warn you, I am no expert.'

'Thank you. I believe there are several other similar romance novels on the shelf in the yellow drawing-room downstairs. Do you wish me to send for them?'

'Perhaps tomorrow. I still have this volume to read.'

When Grace eventually retired she was unable to sleep. She was used to having a more active life, hiding from her step-father had meant she absented herself from the estate as often as possible. She would ride for hours when the weather was clement, spend time visiting the tenants and assisting at the school her mother had established before her sad demise.

Her book was finished, there was nothing else on the shelf that interested her. Then she recalled that there were similar titles in the yellow drawing-room. Although she had been lurking upstairs these past days, on the few occasions she had been able to creep out and walk briskly around the grounds she had spied this particular room. However, this had been from the outside. Would she be able to discover its whereabouts from within?

She had heard the carriage return an hour or more ago, the house was quiet, even the ever-vigilant Foster gone to his bed. Should she risk going downstairs? She was in her night apparel, but her dressing robe had been selected for its comfort and warmth, not elegance. Her hair was loose, she had persuaded Molly to wash it one more time and had been sitting in front of the fire letting it dry whilst she read. She deftly plaited it and tied a ribbon around the end.

Being wide awake, as full of energy as if she'd already slept for several hours, she decided she would take the risk. Lord Shalford had his rooms on the ground floor, they were in the east wing and the chamber she sought was in the central block on the west side. There was no danger of being discovered by him. She wasn't sure where Rupert resided, but would take the chance that

121

he was also sleeping soundly wherever he might be. No doubt he would have imbibed far too much and had fallen between the sheets in his customary inebriated state.

She pushed a taper into the embers and ignited a candle. With this held securely in one hand she ventured out, the corridor was dark but at the corner her illumination was redundant.

Here several wall sconces in the main passageway were still flickering. She hesitated; should she leave her candlestick behind? The heavy silver was decidedly heavy. If the sconces were alight up here, then they would be downstairs as well. She placed her candlestick, still alight, at the corner of the corridor down which she must return. Gathering up her skirts, she ran lightly down the stairs. Which way now? She closed her eyes and tried to visualise exactly where she'd peeped into the room she wished to find. The chamber was at the far side, adjacent to the west wing in which the guest rooms and servants' quarters and necessary offices were housed.

She walked briskly down the central corridor, watching the numerous doors. She was almost certain the yellow drawing-room would be the last door. She opened the door and stopped on the threshold. Botheration! Her wits were addled; of course this room was dark, not even the remains of a fire glowing in the grate. She would have to return and bring down her candlestick after all.

It took her a further quarter of an hour to retrace her steps. She wished she'd left the door ajar, which would make it easier to find. She quickened her steps, the sooner she had something to read and returned the safety of her own rooms the better.

* * *

Ralph had taken papers to his apartment as remaining in the study would mean the staff staying up until he decided to retire. He was working on an urgent estate matter when a faint click alerted him. Was that the door to his foyer opening? He swung back in his chair, tilting his head. No, he must have been mistaken. He tossed his quill on to the blotter; he'd continue this tomorrow morning. He glanced at the tall clock ticking noisily in the far corner of the chamber. A quarter-past one. Time he found his bed.

His lips thinned as he recalled his brother's protestations of undying love for Miss Hadley. He had only prevented the fool from announcing he was married to the assembled diners by threatening to box his ears if he did so. They both knew he would do nothing of the kind, but his younger brother recognised the danger signs.

Ralph stood up, yawned and stretched. He'd long discarded his evening jacket, was in his shirt sleeves and waistcoat, his cravat dangling around his neck. What he would like was a large pot of coffee, but far too late to disturb the kitchen staff. Tonight he would make an exception and go down and fetch it for himself.

He lit a candle and stepped into the vestibule from which all his chambers led. He was about to open the door when he heard footsteps in the passageway outside. It could only mean one thing, there was a burglar abroad. Blowing out his candle, he removed it from the stick and reversed the heavy object, it would be ideal as a weapon. Then he flattened himself against the wall and waited.

The door slowly opened. His jaw dropped. He instantly recognised the outline of the person stepping in. Miss Hadley. A rush of bitter disappointment flooded through him; this was rapidly followed by white hot anger. The girl was still married to his brother and yet here she was seeking him out in his private chambers in the middle of the night.

Stepping into the room Grace held up her candlestick. Her fingers tightened, her knees all but gave way beneath her. This was not the room she wanted. Before she could retreat the door closed quietly behind her.

'Well, well, I was not so far off the mark after all. I take it you're looking for me?'

The candlestick slipped from her fingers and landed on her toes. Despite the shock of finding herself closeted with Lord Shalford the pain in her left foot made her cry out. The chamber was inky black, she crouched down cradling her injured foot.

'Devil take it! Stay where you are, I shall fetch a light.'

Before she could warn him he was upon her, his knees collided painfully with her back, sending her sprawling. Unable to retain his balance he trod painfully on her hand and then crashed against a piece of furniture and joined her on the carpet. Her ears burned from his intemperate language but she was too distressed to complain.

Sibling Rivalry

'Blast! Are you hurt? I heard you cry out.' Grace was unable to answer, he'd quite knocked the breath from her body.

Shalford regained his feet and pushed open a door, flooding the space with light. Then he was on his knees and gently rolled her over. One arm slipped beneath her knees and the other around her shoulders and she was hoisted unceremoniously into the air.

She was still too short of breath to complain that she had no wish to go inside his apartment. Being in his vestibule in her night garments was quite bad enough.

'Don't try and speak, close your mouth and breathe slowly through your nose. I'm going to put you on the sofa.'

She did as he suggested and found her tortured breathing began to ease.

Her head rested on the arm, she closed her eyes, waiting until she was able to speak. He was beside her again, about to remove her slipper and examine her foot. She attempted to snatch it back but the pain was too fierce and she barely held back her moan.

'Please, sir, I don't wish you to . . . it's not seemly . . . we must send for my abigail.'

His touch was gentle and his voice quite different from the sharp tone she was accustomed to. 'I think, my dear, it would be far better if no one was to know of your presence here, even your maid.' His expression changed. 'Good grief! I believe you might have broken one of your toes.'

She winced and immediately he took her hand and examined what was quite obviously the imprint of his boot.

'This is all my fault. I cannot tell you how sorry I am that I have caused you hurt, Miss Hadley. I fear we shall have to summon the physician to take care of these injuries.'

'Right now? In the middle of the night? I would much prefer to wait until the morning. I came down here to . . . '

'To do exactly what?' His enquiry had an edge of steel.

Only then did she recall what he'd said when she first arrived. She felt the heat begin at her toes and slowly creep the length of her body until she was burning all over. 'I came down to collect a book from the yellow drawing-room. Lady Shalford told me there were several recent novels there.'

His eyes lightened and he shook his head in disbelief. 'I take it that geography is not a strong suit of yours? You turned east instead of west, the room you seek is at the other side of the building.'

Mortified, not only at her dismal sense of direction but also that he had believed she'd come to visit him. 'Lord Shalford, could I trouble you to carry me back to my apartment? I shall summon Molly once I am safely there. I shall tell her . . . ' She stopped, not sure how she could explain her injuries, especially the unmistakable imprint of a boot heel on the back of her hand.

'I shall do so at once. Is your maid discreet?' As he spoke he scooped her up for the second time and strode to the door.

'She is. She has been with me since I was a girl. Once my hand is bandaged no-one need know how the injury came about. I shall tell your mama that I fell asleep reading a book and tripped in the dark.'

He whisked her through the deserted house but paused where she had left her lighted candlestick. 'Can you manage to pick that up with your good hand?'

'I can. I shall need it when I reach my sitting-room as I left no illumination there.' Somehow she stretched out and recovered the object without extinguishing the flickering flame. He shouldered his way into her parlour and put her on the divan pushed up against the wall. 'If you could kindly ring the bell before you leave, I should be grateful.'

The bell tinkled and the sound of movement immediately came from the small bedchamber Molly occupied. 'I must bid you good night, my dear, I shall come and see how you are tomorrow.'

'No, you mustn't. How could you possibly be aware that I am injured?'

His smile made her toes curl. 'This is my home, I am fully aware of everything that goes on here.' He disappeared through the door just as Molly bustled in.

'Lawks, whatever next! Look at your poor hand, however did you come to do that?'

'I have also damaged my foot, if you would fetch me cold compresses then I shall tell you the whole story.'

When Grace had completed her tale Molly shook her head. 'Do you think his lordship knows about Lady Shalford and yourself?'

'I think not. My hair is still damp so

will have looked as dark as it did before, and in these old garments I'm sure I look just as dowdy. No, I'm not concerned about his having discovered our secret. My worry is that I shall be unable to go down to dinner tomorrow. Lady Shalford will be so disappointed if we cannot surprise his lordship and his brother as planned.'

Molly finished bathing both injuries. 'I think the damage is not as severe as you feared. If you rest up tomorrow, I reckon you'll be able to walk. Mind you, you will probably have a bit of a limp.'

'Not only that, I shall not be able to wear the matching gloves. They fit so snugly they will not go over the bandage on this hand.'

Molly assisted her to bed, and Grace was ready to sleep. Her dreams were full of a blond-haired, tawny-eyed gentleman — fierce and formidable but very attractive.

Ralph returned to his domain not sure why he felt so unsettled by the encounter with Miss Hadley. It could hardly be her alluring beauty, even in her nightwear she had not raised his pulse one iota. It must be the fact that he'd caused her to drop a heavy silver candlestick on her toes and had compounded this by treading on her hand. However much he might dislike the girl, he was not in the habit of causing a female any distress.

The clock in his study struck two. He might as well get a few hours sleep, although it hardly seemed worth the effort. He was determined to rise at dawn and send a groom to fetch Dr Fletcher. His mouth curved as he imagined the torrent of abuse his younger sibling would heap on his shoulders.

* * *

'Nothing to worry about, Miss Hadley. Severe bruising can be painful but will soon improve. The cold compresses you have worn overnight have been beneficial.' Dr Fletcher smiled benevolently and closed his medical bag.

'I was intending to dine downstairs tonight, Dr Fletcher. Shall I be able to walk without assistance by then?' Grace liked this elderly gentleman, particularly his flamboyant style of dress. He was wearing a waistcoat of gold and green stripes, blue breeches, brown top boots and a bottle green coat.

'I see no reason why you shouldn't, Miss Hadley. Make sure you rest your foot all day, keep it elevated as I've shown you, this will help reduce the swelling. Now, if you will excuse me, I shall call in and see Lady Shalford before I leave.'

Grace hoped that her ladyship had due warning of this visit and was safely ensconced in her armchair and not perambulating about her apartment. The doctor was bound to tell Lord Shalford if he discovered his patient had made a remarkable recovery in the space of less than a week.

'Molly, could you go with the footman to the yellow drawing-room and see if you can find those books. I shall need something to occupy myself if I'm to be marooned on this sofa all day.'

She had just settled herself with the first of these titles, a gothic romance, when Molly was obliged to open the door. A footman staggered in with an enormous arrangement of hothouse flowers, another followed behind with a basket in which were not one, but two, pineapples.

'Put the flowers on the octagonal table in front of the window, Molly. The fruit can go on the side table.' Grace broke the blob of red wax and opened the note that had accompanied these gifts. The bold black writing suited the sender. She quickly scanned the contents not sure if she was offended or pleased by the sentiments it contained.

My dear Miss Hadley,

Kindly accept these small tokens in the hope that they will add weight to my apologies.

I understand from Dr Fletcher that

you have suffered no fractures and for this I am profoundly grateful.

I'm sure that you have no wish to remain under this roof any longer than is necessary. I must warn you that Rupert has decided he wishes to make the marriage genuine. You will not be surprised to know that I have told him it will be over my dead body. I remain your obedient servant.

The indecipherable scrawl at the end of the letter must be his signature.

Soft footsteps approached the door and to her astonishment Lady Shalford peaked around. 'I had to come and see you, dearest girl, I do hope you are not suffering too badly from your accident.' Her eyes widened and she caught sight of the flowers and fruit. 'Are these from Rupert by any chance?'

Grace laughed. 'They are from Ralph. He takes his duties as master of the house very seriously it would seem.' She shuddered theatrically. 'I dread to think what Rupert might send me when he hears of my injuries.'

'He was in his cups last night, I doubt he'll make an appearance until lunchtime. I am so looking forward to this evening, such a shame you won't be able to wear the entire ensemble Madame Ducray has provided. Shall you be able to put on the matching slippers?'

'I sincerely hope so for I have nothing else suitable. As they are heeled I shall have to wear both or none at all. Fortunately without them my gown is long enough to cover my feet. I'm hoping that with the gold silk stockings on it will not be immediately obvious I'm without slippers.'

'Another thing, my dear, I think it is high time we abandoned the formalities. I should like you to use my given name, it's Sarah. In future I shall call you Grace.'

'Are you quite sure you wish me to address you so casually? Shalford will disapprove.'

'Fiddlesticks to that; we are friends, are we not? What is more natural than using our first names.'

Grace changed the subject. 'I hope that you were able to disguise your remarkable improvement from the doctor, Sarah.'

'Indeed. I complained bitterly about the aches and pains and how miserable I was. He will have reported to Ralph, so this will make tonight so much more exciting.'

Sarah came over and kissed Grace on the brow. 'I must return to my rooms, the surprise will be quite spoilt if Ralph appears and I'm not there.'

The day passed pleasantly enough and Grace pushed aside her worries about the coming evening. She wasn't sure Lord Shalford would take kindly to further surprises which involved herself. A bubble of excitement bubbled up inside her. If she was being honest she wanted to look her best. Neither Rupert nor his brother had seen her looking anything but dull.

It was at exactly half-past six when Molly stood back. 'There miss, you look as pretty as a picture. That gown is perfect with your colouring.' Her maid shook her head. 'It's a right shame you can't wear the gloves or the slippers.'

Grace glanced down at her stockinged toes. 'I pray that no-one else will notice the discrepancy. I don't believe I've ever had such a lovely gown.' She smoothed the golden yellow silk between her fingers. 'I'm not sure about the neckline, even with these delightful rosebuds, is it not too low?'

'Lawks, miss, it's just right. I reckon you think you're revealing a bit too much because you're not used to wearing pretty clothes. The pearls are perfect.'

'Yes, thank you for threading them through my hair. If my foot was not so sore I would feel like dancing.' Grace picked up the reticule and fan which had been made to accompany the gown and adjusted the matching gossamer wrap. 'I shall not need you again tonight, Molly. You may take the rest of the evening for yourself.'

Sarah clapped her hands when Grace entered her sitting-room. 'Dearest Grace, you look spectacular. I knew there was a pretty girl hiding under that disguise but I had no idea just how lovely you are until now. I see you're limping, so this evening it shall be my arm that supports you and not the other way around.'

★ ★ ★

'Rupert, you will wear a hole in the carpet. For heaven's sake, take a glass of champagne and sit down.' Ralph hid his smile as his brother sprawled into a chair. 'Miss Hadley will be down momentarily. Remember what I said to you last night; you will not mention anything that might embarrass our guest.'

'She's my wife. We've not signed the papers yet, until then I shall decide how I speak to her.'

Rupert sounded determined to press ahead with his nonsensical scheme to consummate the union. Ralph glared at his brother. Grace would never become Rupert's true wife.

'I heard from London this morning. Our lawyer is confident he can expedite matters; he will be arriving with the necessary legal documents next week some time. I can assure you Miss Hadley is as determined as I to terminate your relationship.'

The double doors to the grand salon in which he stood had been left open. From his position, lounging against the mantelshelf, he couldn't see the stairs. His brother was better placed for this. Rupert's eyes rounded. The crystal glass slipped from his fingers, spilling the contents on the priceless carpet.

What now? Ralph stepped away from the fire. His own drink slopped down his immaculate grey silk waistcoat. Walking smoothly across the entrance hall was Mama, miraculously recovered from her injuries; beside her was the most beautiful creature he had ever set eyes on. A second or two passed before he realised this enchanting young lady was Miss Hadley, somehow transformed from a plain, shapeless dowd into the woman of his dreams.

Somehow Grace had negotiated the staircase without mishap. It had been all but impossible to manage her bag, fan, hold up her skirts and place her injured toes so they did not give way beneath her.

Rupert was slumped in a chair; his reaction to their appearance was everything it should be. Then Lord Shalford stepped into view. She almost tripped. His incredulous expression as he gazed at her sent a flicker up her spine. His eyes darkened, he appeared not to have noticed Sarah at her side. His full attention was on her, she wasn't sure she was ready to deal with his obvious admiration.

Rupert leapt to his feet and pushed past his brother. 'Grace, I can't tell you how pleased I am to see you.' He nodded at his mother. 'Good to see you on your feet again, Mama.' He grabbed at Grace's hand, intending to pull it through his arm. Unfortunately he gripped the damaged one.

Sarah diffused the tension. 'Boys, have you nothing to say to your mama? Here I am, on my own two feet, downstairs to dine with you for the first time in months and you have eyes only for my companion.'

Grace saw both men pause as they understood the significance of having their mother with them. Lord Shalford was the first to react, as one would expect. He strode forward and swept his mother up into a hug, swinging her around as if she were a child and not a mature lady in her late forties.

'Mama, you are right to chide us. We should have been celebrating your miraculous recovery and not allowed ourselves to be bowled over by Miss Hadley.' He set his mother down and Rupert immediately embraced her. Shalford then turned his attention to her. 'Whatever I say you will no doubt take umbrage, my dear. If I tell you how lovely you look tonight, will you think I am casting aspersions on your former appearance?'

He was quite irresistible when being charming. Grace returned his smile and without a second thought placed her hand on his arm when he offered it. 'I expect you are baffled by this sudden change in me. Suffice it to say that for the past three years I have been obliged to disguise myself, your mother persuaded me to come out of hiding.'

'I'm relieved to see you've suffered no permanent damage from your accident last night.' His eyes widened as he looked at her feet. She felt the muscles of his arm clench beneath her fingers. 'God's teeth! You have no slippers on.' His exclamation of surprise carried to Rupert and Sarah.

'No shoes? Why ever not? And what is this about an accident?' Rupert abandoned his mother and came to stand an arm's length from Grace.

'I fell asleep in my parlour and tripped and fell in the darkness. I apologise for my improper attire, but I could not fit my damaged toes into my slipper.' Whilst speaking she attempted to slide her hand from Shalford's arm but for some reason he clamped his own across hers and was refusing to let her move away.

'Ralph, I think I should escort Grace. After all she is my wife.'

Grace was not comfortable being bickered over like two dogs with a bone. 'Shalford, kindly release me. I intend to go in to dine with Sarah.' She wasn't sure if her unexpected use of his mother's given name or the fact that she wasn't going to walk with his younger brother upset him, but immediately he removed his hand and stepped aside with a polite bow.

'Foster is about to announce dinner, I am so excited to be down after being so long closeted in my chambers.' Sarah smiled at Grace and took her arm. There was a decided chill in the air as they sailed forward, leaving the gentlemen to escort each other. 'Ralph is decidedly put out, dearest girl, he's not used to trailing along behind. As the master of this establishment it is his right to walk in first and he should be escorting me.'

'Then he must do so.' Before Sarah could disagree Grace stepped to one side and curtsied to Shalford, who was close behind her. For a second she thought she detected admiration in his eyes, and then his haughty stare returned. 'I beg your pardon, my lord, you must take precedence.'

He nodded and immediately stepped round her and took his mother's arm leaving her to proceed either on her own or with Rupert. He seemed to have lost interest in the matter. She was given no option and found herself linked firmly to his younger brother who smiled at her. His expression was definitely adoring and Grace wasn't certain which was worse; being disdained or being idolised.

Foster bowed them into the dining-room, a bewigged footman stood to attention behind each chair. The table was large enough to seat fifty and for some reason Foster had seen fit to place them at equal distances around the edge. She would be isolated in a sea of silver cutlery and crystal glassware, would need to shout in order to converse with her fellow diners.

No-one else seemed to think this was ridiculous. Sarah was guided to the place at one end of the table, Shalford marched back and took the one opposite his mama. This meant not only would she be sitting on her own on the longest side, she would also be hidden from Rupert by an enormous silver epergne filled with similar flowers to those she had in her bed chamber.

The only thing she recalled about the meal when the final covers were removed was that there had been at least three courses and each one of them enough to feed a small army. So much food quite put her off and she found she was only able to pick at the delicacies her attentive footman placed on her plate.

They ate in silence; the others knew better than to do something as vulgar as shout down the length of the table. She saw Sarah nod to her before standing. 'We shall leave you to your port, boys. We eagerly await your arrival in the grand salon.'

It had been impossible to see how much Rupert had consumed during dinner. However her eyes had frequently turned to Lord Shalford and, she was pleased to note, he drank no more than three glasses of claret. Twice she discovered his gaze fixed on her, his expression enigmatic. She left the table not sure if she was admired or disapproved of.

As soon as the door closed behind them she stepped forward and took Sarah's arm. 'Is that how you always take your dinner? Small wonder you wished to remain in your chambers for the past few months.'

'Whatever do you mean, Grace? Was

the food not excellent? The service impeccable? I believe we keep the finest table in the neighbourhood.'

Hastily Grace explained, she had no wish to be thought ungrateful or critical. 'No, the food was exceptional. It's the fact that you eat in the dining-room at all I find remarkable. Why not use a smaller room? If tradition demands that you take your meals in that huge room, surely it would be far pleasanter to sit at one end of the table so you could converse and not eat in silence?'

'What a quaint idea. This is how it's always been done at Shalford, it would break Foster's heart to compromise in any way.'

'In which case I shall say no more, but I do not intend to join you for dinner again. Delicious as the food was, I scarcely ate a mouthful, I was too tense.'

'Fustian, my dear girl. Ralph will expect you to appear promptly every evening you reside at Shalford. Why else did I purchase you a wardrobe of beautiful evening gowns?'

Grace bit back her sharp retort. She was in an invidious position, neither fish nor fowl; legally part of the family but in fact little more than tiresome guest as far as the head of the household was concerned. Then her heart skipped a beat as she remembered his stunned expression when he had first seen her this evening.

Fortunately her lack of response was not noticed and Sarah filled the silence with her chatter. 'I asked you, my love, if you are a pianist?'

'I beg your pardon, I was wool-gathering. Yes, I am proficient on the pianoforte. Shall I play something for you?' Grace pulled out the piano stool. She ran her fingers over the keys; the instrument had a mellow tone and was perfectly in tune. Music had been her solace in the dark months following her mother's untimely death and without conscious thought she was playing a familiar prelude. She had quite forgotten the piece was supposed to be something for Sarah.

When the last notes faded from the room she was startled to hear a round of applause from behind her. She looked over her shoulder to see Shalford, Rupert and Sarah in a semicircle a few yards away with identical expressions of appreciation.

'That was quite beautiful, Miss Hadley, I had no idea you were so talented.' His lordship nodded encouraging her to continue. 'Please continue, I could listen to you all evening.'

Rupert chimed in. 'Could you play something a bit more cheerful? What about one of those waltzes?'

'I am sadly out of practice, but will attempt one waltz for you all. I thought we could perhaps have a hand or two of cards until the tea trolley arrives?' Not waiting for a response she launched into a lively tune and when finished closed the lid firmly and stood up.

Rupert moved closer, he took her hand and stared earnestly into her face.

'I wish to speak to you on a matter of urgency, my dear Grace. Can I persuade you to take a turn around the room so we can talk privately?'

In any other house this would have been a nonsensical suggestion, but at Shalford Hall the grand salon ran the full length of the central block. One almost needed a spyglass to see from one end to the other, small wonder the chamber was decidedly chilly even with three fires burning brightly. She doubted even in August this chamber would be warm.

She glanced across and saw Sarah talking to her oldest son; with his attention elsewhere it would be safe to accept Rupert's invitation. She had every intention of explaining to him the marriage must be ended, that she had no feelings for him apart from friendship and he must forget this notion that he was in love with her.

'Very well, there is something most particular I wish to say to you as well.' She didn't take the arm he offered, preferring to walk beside him freely. 'I want to make it clear I intend to sign the papers, have the marriage dissolved, and then leave here. It's doubtful we will meet again, for I don't move in the same circles as you and Lord Shalford.'

He seemed unabashed by her blunt remarks. 'I'm not a fool, Grace. I don't expect you to feel the same way as I do, at least not yet. I have come here in the hope I can change your mind. Mama insists you're part of the family now, her dearest friend and companion and she won't hear of you leaving even if the marriage is dismantled.'

She was about to deny this statement when Sarah called out from the far end of the room. 'Come along, Ralph has set up the table and we are to play cards as you suggested, Grace.'

This particular game involved gambling and was certainly not what she had in mind. Rupert quickened his pace, leaving her to walk behind him. Sarah was already seated, Shalford, as was correct, on his feet. 'I'm afraid that

153

I don't play games of chance, my lord, so if you will excuse me I'll return to my chambers. My hand and foot have become decidedly uncomfortable.'

Rupert ignored her statement, and the fact that she was standing, and pulled out a chair, his eyes burning with the fervour of a hardened gambler. Then she understood. Shalford had suggested the game in order to remind her of his brother's frailty. His stratagem was unnecessary; she would not be in this invidious position was it not for a wager.

'We shall only be playing for small stakes, my dear, do come and join us,' Sarah said, patting the chair next to hers.

'Forgive me, but I am poor company at the moment. Dr Fletcher gave me strict instructions to rest my foot for a day or two, I fear I have overdone it.' She wished then that she had exaggerated her limp.

Instantly his lordship stepped forward and, before she could move aside, he picked her up. 'In which case, Miss Hadley, I shall return you to your rooms. I would not dream of allowing you to attempt the staircase.'

'Put me down at once, sir, I'm quite capable of walking, and well you know it,' she said sharply.

Ignoring her protests he strode off as if she weighed no more than a bag of feathers. He all but galloped up the stairs and walked into her sitting-room as if he belonged there. He deposited her on the divan and stepped hastily away as if expecting her to retaliate with violence.

This made her smile and she recalled the incident when they'd first met. 'My lord, I don't believe I ever apologised sufficiently for striking you. I can assure you such behaviour is quite out of character and will not occur again.'

His mouth curved and suddenly he looked more approachable, like a gentleman she could perhaps like. 'I am relieved to hear you say so, Miss Hadley.' He half bowed and strolled to the open door before completing his sentence. 'For I can assure you if it did happen again you would regret it.'

He leant nonchalantly against the door, smiling in a way that might have been mistaken for flirtatious.

She stepped back two paces, his heat pulsed from him.

He straightened. 'Do you ride, Miss Hadley?'

His unexpected question took her by surprise and she answered truthfully. 'I do. Music and horses are my greatest loves.'

'In which case you shall ride with me as soon as you are able to. I have the perfect mount in my stables, a pretty grey mare.' He smiled lazily, but instead of stepping away he stepped closer and, tilting her chin in one strong hand, he pressed his lips lightly against hers.

She could hear his laughter echoing down the passage way as he strode away. He was quite impossible. Just when she thought she understood him he behaved quite out of character.

The Truth Is Revealed

Next morning dawned bright and clear and Grace discovered the swelling on her foot and hand had gone down sufficiently to wear both boots and gloves. She intended to take Shalford up on his offer of a mount, a gallop around the park was exactly what she needed to clear her head.

'Molly, I shall need my riding habit. I don't want my morning chocolate today as I shall breakfast when I return.'

'You're happy today, miss. You beginning to like it here, then?' Molly asked as she held out the various items her mistress needed to complete her toilette.

Grace could hardly tell her abigail her first real kiss was what had raised her spirits. For the past few years she had wondered what it would be like to experience a man's lips on hers, now she knew.

Then her happiness drained away. Only when a man was betrothed to a lady was he allowed to kiss her. The ladies who were kissed in other circumstances were no better than flirts or even worse. Shalford had taken advantage of her. She was legally married to his brother — what he had done was shameful.

'Could you make sure that Lady Shalford knows my whereabouts? I shall visit her after I have breakfasted.' She glanced at the array of gowns Molly had draped over a wooden rail for her inspection. 'I shall wear the russet, it has a pretty neckline and long sleeves. I expect to be gone at least an hour, I should like to bathe when I return.'

As the hour was early there was no sign of either Shalford or Rupert. In fact she was certain she spotted two parlour maids with dusters whisking round a corner as she descended the staircase. The fires were lit, the vast central hall quite warm. It must cost a fortune to keep a house of this size comfortable during the winter months if the place was so cold in April. She hesitated, she was sure there must be a more direct route to the stables than using the front door. She was about to pull a nearby bell-strap when she heard steps approaching.

'Good morning, Miss Hadley. Excellent, you shall accompany me this morning. Might I be permitted to say how attractive your habit is? The colour is the exact shade of your hair now that hideous dye has been removed.'

She wanted to put him in his place. Make sure he knew he could not trifle with her affections but his warm smile prevented her sharp retort. 'Good morning, my lord, I did not expect to see you at this time.' She wished her comment unsaid, it sounded suspiciously like she was not pleased to see him. 'I mean . . . '

'My dear girl, I know exactly what you meant. I've not been the easiest of companions, but henceforth I shall be pleasant and polite.'

'You, my lord, are quite impossible.' She smiled at him. She could not remain aloof when he was charming. 'I believe it must be so long since you were pleasant, polite or teasing you have not quite got the feel of it yet.'

His shout of laughter startled an unfortunate footman and the tray of cutlery he was carrying crashed to the floor. Grace wanted to assist him to collect it is it had been her fault it had been dropped, but Shalford took her arm and escorted her firmly past the accident and out of the side door she had been searching for.

'It does not do to interfere with the staff in their duties, Miss Hadley, far better to let them do what they're paid handsomely for.'

Grace snatched her arm from his hand. 'I don't need lessons from you, my lord, in how to behave with servants. I doubt you, from your lofty position at the head of the household, are aware how strict your butler is. That poor young man could well lose his position because of us.'

She hurried away towards the sound of buckets clanking and horses munching. Thank goodness the stables were not far from the rear of the house. Then her path was blocked by a solid wall of flesh. She stopped so suddenly her injured toes were pressed against her boot and she yelped, falling forward in her distress.

Her tumble was prevented by his intervention. 'Devil take it! Let me carry you back to the house, sweetheart, I should have realised your foot is not sufficiently recovered to be riding.'

Pushing herself away from his embrace, she shook her head vehemently. 'You shall do no such thing, Shalford. Kindly remove yourself from my path before you do me further injury.' The use of the endearment had not gone unnoticed.

'As you wish. Might I be allowed to beg your pardon yet again? I cannot think why I am so maladroit in your company.' His lopsided smile diffused her irritation.

'It's strange you should say so, for I am famous for my even temper and yet I have been at daggers drawn with you on several occasions.'

At this point they reached the stable yard and to her astonishment the grey mare, which he had mentioned last night, was saddled and ready alongside a massive black stallion. The horse was cavorting and sidling, lifting the unfortunate stable boy from his feet as he did so. How could the grooms have known she was to come down this morning? Puzzled, she turned to Lord Shalford. 'Are your staff clairvoyant, sir?'

He chuckled. 'It would appear so, but I will admit I heard you descending the stairs and sent a footman out to warn them. What do you think of the mare? Her name's Silver Star. As you no doubt observed, she's a spirited animal. My mother used to enjoy her antics.'

Grace moved forward, hand out-stretched and the horse lowered her head and nuzzled it. 'What a pretty girl. You and I are going to be such friends.' She glanced over her shoulder before continuing. 'Thank you for believing I am indeed an expert horsewoman.'

She gathered the reins, gripped the pommel and turned, bending her leg so that a groom could toss her into the saddle. Instead her boot was grasped by his lordship. As she settled herself, hooking her knee over the pommel, adjusting her habit and ramming her boot into the stirrup, he was vaulting on to his massive beast.

The two animals scattered the remaining grooms by their plunging. Grace laughed, there was nothing she liked more than an exciting ride. By the time they were on the greensward both animals were progressing in a more sedate manner. She could not help noticing what an excellent seat he had, how magnificent he looked astride his stallion.

To her consternation his head turned and their eyes met. She could see he reciprocated her feelings of admiration. 'Is it safe to gallop? I think Silver needs to stretch her legs.'

'I have a mile or more of park land and it's excellent going today. Why not enjoy ourselves?'

Grace touched her heel to Silver's side and the mare leapt forward, if she'd not been prepared she would have been flung from the saddle. Leaning forward she relaxed the reins allowing the animal to find her own pace. They thundered down the grass, the wind whipped tears from her eyes and her smart military style cap flew from her head and her hair came loose from its pins.

Shalford's stallion surged past, sending huge divots into the air, one of which hit her on the side of the head, blinding her for a moment. By the time she scraped away the mud he was fifty yards ahead of her. This would not do at all. She crouched over Silver's neck and urged her faster.

The mare responded and yard by yard began to overhaul the black horse, but just as Silver's nose came level with his boot he glanced sideways. Immediately he flicked his reins and once again Grace was showered with mud.

The brick wall which bounded the park was rapidly approaching, the race was over. She sat back in her saddle pulling gently on the reins delighted by the instant response she got from the mare. Soon they were in a collected canter, then a trot and finally walking. Silver was breathing evenly, in no distress from their mad dash.

Shalford reined in and trotted back to her, his smile made her catch her breath. 'Well, sweetheart, that was exhilarating. I fear Caliban has covered you with mud, and your hair has come down.' He delved into his pocket and produced a pristine white square and handed it to her.

'Thank you for pointing this out to

me. I hadn't been aware of the massive clods of mud that hit me full in the face.' Smiling, she wiped the worst of it from her cheeks and sensibly refrained from returning the item to its owner. 'I've also lost my hat, perhaps we could look out for it on our return?' She attempted to gather up her hair one-handed but failed dismally.

'Allow me, my mount has been trained to stand if I drop the reins on his neck.' Without a by-your-leave he edged closer until they were boot to boot and reached out to gather up her wayward locks. She found it hard to remain stationary; having his gloved hands move back and forth across her face and neck was almost too much to bear. She felt pins being removed and stabbed back in.

'There, it's more or less up, but I doubt it would stay put if we were to gallop again.'

'I think one race is enough for Silver, after all she hasn't been ridden much lately.' She carefully patted her head; it seemed secure enough for the moment. 'Where are we going next? I should like to see more of the grounds if that's possible.'

For a moment she thought he was going to take her hand, then he swung his horse around and pointed into the distance. 'Over there is Mama's Folly, would you like to see it? There's a splendid view of the ornamental lake and the house from there.'

It took a quarter-of-an hour to reach the pink marble monstrosity. Grace shook her head in disbelief at the cherubs, fishes and mythical beasts that crawled all over the edifice. He swung down from the saddle and tethered his horse to a metal ring then returned to lift her easily from the saddle.

'I can see you are lost for words, Miss Hadley. No, I refuse to keep calling you Miss Hadley when you are all but a member of the family. I notice you now address my mother by her given name, might I have the privilege of using yours?'

'No doubt you will use it anyway, permission or not. I think I prefer to continue addressing you more formally, after all we have only been acquainted a week.'

'I think it's rather too late to be worrying about propriety, sweetheart. My name is Ralph, I should be honoured if you would call me that and not address me as Shalford or my lord.'

Her cheeks coloured at his pointed reference to what had taken place the previous evening. Did he not realise he had compromised her? She was grateful she could hide her discomposure by busying herself tethering her own mount to a second metal ring.

When she finished he vanished behind the building. She loosened Silver's girth and patted her neck pleased to see the animal was already cool. 'I shall be down every morning to give you exercise and soon I shall know every inch of this estate.'

He spoke from right behind her, startled she stepped back and received a deluge of water for her trouble. 'Botheration! Now my habit is quite soaked. I wish you would not creep behind a person in that way.'

Chuckling he placed a full pail in front of each of the horses. 'There's sweet hay in the back, you might as well come and collect some, you are so dishevelled it can hardly make a difference now.'

Obviously Sarah had been used to coming to this building on a regular basis for there to be fodder and water for the horses kept here. 'Is the water safe to drink? I believe I swallowed a considerable amount of mud earlier.'

A further quarter-of-an hour passed before the horses were taken care of, warm blankets thrown over their backs and a pile of hay in front of them. He held out his hand and she took it. It would seem churlish not to in the circumstances. He tucked it through his arm and led her around to the front.

'Come. Mama always keeps a selection of refreshments here. A groom comes out and replenishes them most days.' He grinned at her sceptical expression. 'I know, sweetheart, he would hardly have done so these past few months. However, I set things in motion yesterday. I had a feeling we would be calling here today.'

She giggled. 'I believe it is the lord and master who is clairvoyant here, not the staff.' She dropped his arm and ran lightly up the steps. Inside there was a fire lit, a table laid for two and, to her astonishment, freshly baked rolls, strawberry conserve, butter and a large pot of steaming coffee. 'Breakfast? This is a perfect end to a delightful excursion.'

Whilst she was biting into her roll it occurred to her she was unchaperoned. She lowered the tasty morsel and stared at the gentleman sitting, relaxed and smiling, opposite her. 'You do realise I should not be here with you? Society would frown upon this alfresco meal.'

His eyes crinkled endearingly at the corners as he smiled. 'Don't fuss, Grace. I am your brother-in-law, who could possibly object to us being unattended?'

'I don't understand. I came here to have the marriage annulled as I have no wish to be tied to your brother. You were adamant the union must be terminated and you have, until yesterday, been referring to me as Miss Hadley. To now claim kinship in order to make this clandestine meeting acceptable is too much.'

He raised his coffee cup in salute. 'I know and you know your marriage is a sham, but until the lawyers produce the necessary papers you are legally Rupert's wife. Therefore I am your brother-in-law and we can breakfast together with no fear of offending Society.'

Grace was far too hungry to debate the point, if he was content then so should she be.

Eventually she was full and wiped her sticky fingers and mouth on a napkin. 'That was quite delicious. And even more extraordinary is the fact that we have conversed without argument the entire time.' She stood up, shaking the crumbs from her habit.

He leaned over and his fingers closed around her hand. Her heart fluttered. He was going to kiss her again, but instead he released her and turned away. 'We must get on or the horses will become chilled. It is inclement for the time of year.'

* * *

Ralph marched down the stairs. Stepping aside was the most difficult thing he'd done in his life. Every instinct made him want to take her in his arms, to kiss her breathless, but she was not his. He must put his own feelings aside in the interests of his brother's welfare. Both he and his mother wanted Rupert to join the army, thus providing routine and stability to rid him of his demons. The marriage must stand until Grace had weaned him from his unpleasant cronies. The thought that during this

172

period she might fall in love with his brother was tearing him apart.

* * *

The ride back was uneventful, but Grace was aware Ralph had withdrawn from her; he was once again the haughty aristocrat. He was as aware as she there could be nothing between them, but she had begun to believe he viewed her differently.

She frowned at the back of his head. He was riding slightly ahead of her as the long stride of his stallion made it difficult for her mare to keep up unless she jogged. She reviewed the events of the past few days. She suspected his interest in her had not commenced until after she appeared in a beautiful gown and restored to her normal appearance. What went on inside a person was more important, in her opinion; however beautiful they were, or what garments they were decked out in should make no difference to how

173

they were perceived.

Being cross with him was a more familiar sensation than those she had been experiencing since last night. Far safer to dislike him and push her growing feelings firmly to one side. She kicked Silver into a canter and arrived at his side in a rush. 'My lord, I forgot to mention I shall not be dining with you in future.'

His eyes flashed and his mouth curved down. 'Is there something you dislike about the food, or is it the company you wish to avoid?' His question was bland, his expression watchful. He reined in and swung in his saddle in order to face her.

'The food is excellent, the company also.' She saw puzzlement in his eyes and smiled at his confusion. 'No, I spoke to your mother about the problem but she insisted things can't be changed.'

'Devil take it! You're talking in riddles. What is it you wish me to alter so that you will join us for dinner?'

'I refuse to sit on my own with several yards of empty table on either side of me unable to converse. I suggested we eat in a smaller room, or perhaps laid all four places at one end of the table, but it seems Foster would be put out if we did so.'

'Foster will have to get used to it. I can't think why I've allowed things to continue in this ridiculous fashion. You're quite right to point it out to me. I promise you in future we shall dine somewhere more comfortable.' He smiled at her and her heart did strange things. 'Do I have your promise you will join us tonight and every other night?'

'You do. After all if I'm not around to talk to Rupert I shall have no opportunity to persuade him to purchase his colours.'

'Exactly so; I had been about to say the very same thing myself.'

They clattered into the stable yard and further conversation was impossible. She waited for him to lift her down from the saddle but he strode off in the direction of the house leaving this task to a groom.

That night she took extra time to prepare herself. Further evening gowns, promenade dresses, spencers and pelisses had arrived that afternoon. It had been difficult to select a favourite, she'd never owned more than two evening gowns at one time.

'The gold silk with the spangled overdress is right for you, miss, autumn shades suit you best if you don't mind my saying so.'

Grace examined her reflection in the long glass and was pleased with what she saw. 'As the gown has short sleeves I shall take the wrap. It's fortunate I can now wear the gloves and evening slippers. I felt decidedly uncomfortable without either last night.'

'I can't credit how quickly your hair has returned to its natural golden brown, miss, real pretty it looks in the candlelight.'

'I must go. Lady Shalford and I are going down together again. I shall need my habit tomorrow; will it be ready to wear?'

'I'll get on to it right away. I'll leave it out for you, shall I? I reckon you'll be up with the lark and gone before I can bring in your chocolate and rolls.'

Sarah was waiting and looked quite lovely in a deep blue evening gown, the neck, cuffs and hem decorated with darker blue bugle beads. A magnificent sapphire necklace and matching ear-bobs completed her outfit. 'My dear, I do believe tonight's gown is even more becoming than the other one. I see you have your slippers and gloves on. I think that's why you were so tense last night. Nothing at all to do with the arrangement of the table.'

Grace thought it better not to mention there was to be a new arrangement tonight, Sarah might misconstrue the fact Ralph had changed a centuries old tradition at her request.

★ ★ ★

Ralph watched Rupert meander around the grand salon unable to settle, he was delighted to see his brother not cradling his customary glass of alcohol. 'Mama and Grace won't be long, they are both excellent timekeepers.'

'I say, have matters improved between you, then? I never expected to hear you use her given name so soon, normally you're a stickler for etiquette.'

'I've decided to give your marriage a chance, although contracted in a most dubious way, especially by you, I think Grace will be a good influence on you. Exactly what you need at the moment.' His brother's face lit with a smile of such intense happiness Ralph knew he'd done the right thing.

All he had to do was convince Grace to let the union stand at least until his brother could be convinced to join the cavalry or had given up his dubious friends and other bad habits. He prayed she would not wish to continue the arrangement after the agreed six months.

'You're a capital fellow, the best brother anyone could have. She doesn't love me, you know, but I'll do me best to convince her she'd be better off with me than on her own.'

'Ah, here they come . . . ' Ralph's words trailed away as the woman he'd fallen irrevocably in love with descended the stairs in a delightful confection of gold silk and sparkly material. Rupert brushed past him and rushed over to greet her.

'Grace, you look pretty tonight. Dashed fine colour that gown is. Do you notice I'm not drinking? I've given it up.'

Mama drifted towards him, it was some consolation to have her restored to full health, he must concentrate on that and not dwell on what might have been. 'Mama, you look enchanting as always. You will be surprised to see I have arranged for us to dine in the blue room. I want to be able to talk to you and Grace whilst we eat.' He kept his tone light, hoping his unhappiness wouldn't be apparent.

She slipped her arm into his and drew him away. 'I see how it is, dearest, I guessed you were smitten when you brought Grace here. Don't look so sad, things have a way of working out for the best. She will soon be free of the entanglement with Rupert and then you can . . . '

'But I can't, Mama. I've decided to let things remain as they are. If Rupert won't become an officer in the cavalry then the only way to save his life from ruination is to let Grace do it. He loves her and would do anything for her.'

Their conversation was interrupted by Foster who appeared looking decidedly put out. 'Dinner is served, my lord, my lady, Miss Hadley and Mr Shalford.' He sighed heavily. 'Tonight you are to dine in the blue room.'

Grace took Rupert's proffered arm. She had enjoyed their conversation, he was a dear boy when not in his cups. The meal was superb but she scarcely noticed what she ate, she was too engrossed in the lively debate between herself and Ralph about the iniquitous Corn Laws which were causing so much distress to country folk. Rupert had but one glass of claret, and remained attentive and loving, although he rarely joined in the conversation.

After dinner she was once more alone with him and he returned to the subject she had tried to avoid. 'Grace, we don't have to wait for the lawyers. Ralph has given us his blessing, why don't we go to my estate as we'd planned? With your help I'm sure I can make it a profitable place.' He smiled and the intensity of his gaze made her feel uncomfortable. 'I'm hoping I can persuade you to make the marriage genuine.'

Flustered, she scrambled to her feet. 'Oh, the tea tray is here. I expect your mother would like me to make it.'

Sarah greeted her affectionately. 'At last, I thought you two young things were going to spend the rest of the evening closeted together.'

Grace glanced across at Ralph but he would not meet her gaze. 'Shall I prepare the tea?'

Rupert joined them and flopped down on the nearest chair, he was relaxed and happy. His brother was quite the opposite. 'Nothing for me, Grace. What about you, Ralph?'

Abruptly he stood up. 'I've just recalled I have an urgent letter to write, it must be taken to catch the mail coach first thing tomorrow.' He bowed politely, bent down to kiss his mother's cheek and strode off.

The evening finished soon after his departure, Rupert escorted her and Sarah to their chambers. 'I shall be joining you first thing tomorrow, Grace, when you take your morning ride.' He grinned ruefully. 'A bit of a shock to the old system, I've not seen an early morning for many a month.'

'I'm proud of you, Rupert. Promise me you'll consider the army life. I think you would make an excellent cavalry officer. Think how smart you would look in red.'

'I don't want to leave you, I'd much prefer to be your husband. Goodnight.' He swayed towards her, intending to kiss her cheek, she quickly stepped away and bid him goodnight from the safety of her parlour.

She couldn't help wishing Ralph would be riding with her tomorrow and not his younger brother. Although this marriage of convenience had seemed the perfect opportunity to escape from Sir John, now she was safe at Shalford she had no wish to continue the charade. As she settled down to sleep something occurred to her. She sat bolt upright.

Good heavens! Ralph had been so withdrawn tonight because he didn't want her to go away with Rupert. There could only be one reason he had given his approval. He was putting his brother's happiness ahead of his own. Her eyes brimmed, everything was such a muddle and she could see no way which could satisfy everyone.

If she had her heart's desire then Rupert's heart would be broken. She was his wife, for whatever reasons and she had spoken her words in the sight of God. Now the circumstances were changed she believed she ought to honour her vows however difficult this was going to be.

The next morning she was heavy eyed and dressed reluctantly. She made her way directly to the stable yard. She had discovered the journey was quicker down the nursery stairs and into the main part of the building. This also meant she was unlikely to meet Ralph; he was so observant he was bound to detect her unhappiness.

Silver Star was more settled this morning; the exercise yesterday had done her good. Rupert rode a splendid chestnut gelding, his seat was excellent. In fact she was forced to admit if she hadn't met Ralph she would be very happy indeed to be married to his brother.

After an hour and a half of cantering and jumping ditches and hedges Rupert decided they should return. 'The lawyer is coming this morning. Have you decided what you wish to do?'

'Yes, I have. I shall let the marriage stand, but only if we leave for your estate tomorrow morning.' Maybe she could bear the separation if she was away from Ralph. She must make sure he understood she had no intention of making it a genuine arrangement. 'Rupert, I must be sure you realise I have not changed my mind about it being a marriage in name only. I shall insist on it being dissolved in a year as we agreed.'

'I am a man of my word. I shall not importune you with my affection but pray you will change your mind.' He smiled. He was the most attractive young man when he was sober. 'However, I'm hoping in time you will come to see me as a suitable partner and return my love in full.'

★ ★ ★

Ralph watched the woman he loved ride away with his brother. He would take his own morning exercise later after he'd spoken to Johnson who was due to arrive at any moment. The lawyer's letter had said he was travelling by post; a hideous expense but it had seemed to be a necessary one a few days ago.

Such extravagance had been a waste of money now the marriage was to stand until the year was over. Having Grace under his roof and not being able to declare his love would become an impossible task the longer she stayed here.

No more than twenty minutes after the two riders vanished into the woodland a post chaise turned on to the drive and bowled towards the house. He left his apartment and headed for the grand salon. Foster greeted him a touch frostily.

'Shall I have refreshments sent in when Mr Johnson arrives, my lord?'

'Do that. Coffee and plum cake will

suffice.' Ralph paced the room, dreading the interview which would mark the end of his hopes. He'd no idea being in love would be such a painful business, for poets only wrote about the joy of the experience.

No-one warned him how it would be agony to be denied the love of your life. Rupert must provide the heir, he would remain a bachelor.

Johnson, a man of middle years, was sharp featured and equally sharp eyed. He was a clever man, not given to hyperbole, reliable and normally unflustered. Today he all but ran towards him. 'My lord, you will not believe what I have discovered.'

★   ★   ★

Rupert lifted Grace from the saddle as easily as Ralph had done. 'Shall we go and give him our good news? I think I saw the lawyer arrive. He's made a wasted journey.'

This time when he took her hand she

did not remove it. As her legal husband he had the right to hold it whenever he wished. A sick dread filled her. What if Rupert started drinking again? Whatever their verbal agreement, legally she was his chattel and must do as he bid or suffer the consequences. She stumbled and he wasn't quick enough to prevent her fall. She crashed painfully to the cobbles. Her head struck the ground and her world went black.

* * *

Ralph shook his head in disbelief. 'Let me get this straight. The priest who conducted the ceremony was bogus? An actor?'

'Indeed he was, my lord. It would appear one of Mr Shalford's more disreputable friends persuaded the man to play the part. No doubt it has caused considerable amusement amongst his cronies.'

'I know my brother is not a keen wit, but to allow himself to be gulled in this way is quite extraordinary.' The rattle of crockery arriving gave him pause. It would not do to discuss the matter in front of any member of staff. Fortunately Grace was still referred to as Miss Hadley, with luck her reputation should remain untarnished by this shocking revelation.

When they were alone again he shook the lawyer vigorously by the hand. 'I can't tell you how relieved I am to get this news. It makes matters so much simpler.'

The sound of running footsteps alerted him. A young footman burst in, his wig askew. 'My lord, you must come at once. Miss Hadley has had an accident.'

Ralph was out of the room in seconds. 'Where is she? Has Foster sent for the physician?'

'Mr Shalford is bringing her inside, she struck her head on the cobbles when she fell and is unconscious. A groom has galloped off to fetch the doctor, my lord.'

He met his brother as he entered the main passageway that led to the central vestibule. Grace was as pale as a ghost, the left side of her face covered in blood. Rupert looked little better.

'Here, let me take her. Go and warn Mama.' Her head flopped horribly against his shoulder as if she was already a corpse. Rupert rushed ahead and the sound of anxious voices greeted Ralph as he carried his precious burden upstairs.

'Take her straight into her bedchamber, Ralph, I shall take care of her now.' His mother stepped up and pressed two fingers against Grace's neck just below her ear, before leading him into the room where the bed had already been turned back. 'Place her carefully. Don't look so worried both of you, her pulse is strong. Head wounds bleed copiously, I'm sure it's not nearly as parlous as it looks.'

Rupert dithered outside the door. 'Come along, there's nothing we can do here. Mama has patched us both up on numerous occasions and knows exactly what to do. There's coffee downstairs and I think we could both do with a brandy to steady our nerves.'

Johnson was waiting anxiously for news. 'How is the young lady, my lord?'

'Not as bad as we feared. Now, Rupert, how did this accident occur?'

His brother explained. 'I couldn't catch her, my drinking has made my reactions slow. It's all my fault.'

It took two cups of heavily sweetened coffee and a large brandy before Rupert was sufficiently calm to be able to hear what to him would be devastating news. When Ralph explained, his reaction was even more extreme than he'd expected. He buried his head in his hands and his shoulders shook. Johnson politely gathered up his papers and made himself scarce.

Ralph put his arm around his sibling to offer comfort. 'Dear boy, do not distress yourself. All is not lost, I shall not stand in your way if you wish to court Miss Hadley.'

Rupert raised a tear-streaked face, looking more like a little boy than a man grown. 'You don't understand. Grace had agreed to come with me, to try to make the marriage work. My stupidity would have ruined her life.' He scrubbed his eyes dry on his sleeve and stood up. 'I cannot bear to face her. I should do what I should have done years ago, become a soldier and learn to be more like you.'

'Don't do anything precipitate, Rupert. You have not known Grace for long, hardly time for her to make up her mind. I see no reason why you shouldn't court her as you intended. I can assure you that you shall have my blessing if you can persuade her to marry you in earnest.'

'She won't wish to speak to me once she knows. But I will remain here until she is well, I couldn't bear to leave without being sure she was going to make a full recovery.'

Ralph gripped his brother's shoulders. 'Good man. None of us wish you to dash off without giving the matter serious thought. If, after you have spoken to Grace, she makes it plain she's not interested then that is the time to consider your options.'

'You are too good to me. I don't deserve your sympathy or support after the way I've been behaving these past two years. The trick my so-called friends played on us was unforgivable. I shall have no dealings with them in future.'

Ralph watched his brother stumble to his apartment. It was going to be torture to stand back and allow Rupert to court the woman he loved. He must give his brother this opportunity whatever his own feelings on the matter.

He could not stay at Shalford. He would go to his estate in the North for a few weeks and give Rupert a clear field. If his brother failed to persuade Grace to become engaged to him after that, then he would be free to stake his own claim. He must pray he was not making the biggest mistake of his life.

An Unexpected Visitor

Grace could hear someone calling her name; they sounded a long way away but were most insistent that she open her eyes. Reluctantly she did so to find Dr Fletcher sitting beside her patting her hand. 'Well, well, my dear girl, you do seem to be a trifle accident prone.'

She attempted to move her head and wished she hadn't. 'Did I knock myself out? How silly of me.'

'You did, but no real harm done. You have a sizeable bruise on your temple, but the cut was not serious enough to require sutures.'

'Do I have to remain in bed to recover?'

He shook his head and beamed at her. 'Not at all, you may get up later today if you wish to. You were only stunned. In fact, you recovered consciousness some time ago but immediately fell asleep. I take it you did not have a restful night last night?'

'I didn't, but apart from a thumping headache I feel perfectly well. I should like to get up right away.' She glanced down and realised she was in her nightgown. 'Perhaps I could ask you to ring for my abigail, sir?'

Molly bustled in clucking like a mother hen. 'Lawks! Whatever next? What with you tripping over and Lord Shalford demanding for his trunks to be packed it's been a right to-do this morning.'

'Ralph is leaving? Are you quite sure, Molly?'

'I'm certain, miss, Lady Shalford and Mr Shalford were talking about it. Now, her ladyship asked to be told as soon as you were awake.'

'Don't send the message yet, Molly, I wish to get up. I expect I'll have a black eye, but that can't be helped, it could have been a lot worse.'

In less than three quarters of an hour she was freshly gowned and ready to go downstairs, her hair arranged in such a way that it almost disguised the injury. Rupert and Sarah were in the grand salon and she decided to join them. She wasn't an invalid and had no wish to be visited in her chambers.

She wished to find out what was driving Ralph away without even waiting to say goodbye. It must be an urgent business matter. On her way she passed Foster who actually smiled and bowed, she almost curtsied in return. He was such an impressive gentleman, far too grand for a mere butler. The murmur of voices drifted into the entrance hall.

Pausing in the open doorway to steady herself, she felt a tad dizzy after her rush down the long staircase. Immediately Rupert was at her side.

'Grace, whatever are you doing down here? You should have remained in your chamber.'

'I am perfectly well, thank you, Rupert.' He looked decidedly sombre and her heart sunk to her slippers.

'What is wrong? Why are you both looking so sombre?'

'I have something serious to tell you, and I pray you don't hate me when you hear the news.'

When he had finished she was all but speechless. 'We're not married at all? The ceremony was a hoax?'

'Yes, I'm afraid so. I cannot tell you how sorry I am. I shall do everything in my power to make it up to you.'

He guided her to the nearest chair and she was grateful for his support. Her legs felt decidedly wobbly. She realised how lucky she was; if they had left Shalford Hall she would have been ruined and obliged to marry Rupert whether she wished it or not. She closed her eyes and was relieved to hear him leave the room.

'You may sit up again, dearest girl, we are alone. Rupert intends to become a cavalry officer and give up his rackety life style. Unfortunately Ralph left before Rupert made his decision known.'

'Why did he go, Sarah? I thought he would be delighted at the news.' She swallowed the lump in her throat, unable to go on.

'He felt it better to be away from Shalford for a while and give you and Rupert time to get to know each other. I had not known him to be so altruistic and wish on this occasion he had put his scruples to one side.'

A glimmer of hope surged through her. 'Are you saying, Sarah, Ralph feels the same way that I do?'

'I should hope he does, my dear. Otherwise his behaviour towards you would be outrageous. I tried to tell him however long he was away it would make no difference, you would never agree to marry Rupert.'

'I should think not. He is not ready for marriage, he is far too immature. Far better for him to buy his colours and have some excitement in his life.'

Sarah rushed across the room and embraced her. 'My darling girl, that is exactly what I hoped to hear you say.

You do love Ralph, don't you?'

'With all my heart; it will be the longest few weeks of my life waiting for him to return.'

'Fiddlesticks to that! I will send after him immediately. I shall have to explain to my youngest son he is chasing moonshine if he thinks to persuade you to love him. He is well aware of your feelings.'

'In which case, I shall take a stroll in the grounds. For once the weather is clement and more like early spring today. I promise I shan't go far.'

'There is a delightful summerhouse where you can rest. If you are not returned within the hour I shall send someone out to look for you.'

She had just stepped into the entrance hall when her heart skipped a beat. She came face to face with the man she loved. 'Ralph, I thought you had gone.' He looked a trifle dishevelled, not his normal immaculate self at all.

'I came back — I found I couldn't

leave without speaking to you first.'

She swayed and he snatched her up.

'Sweetheart, you should not even be up.'

'Thank you for your concern, but Dr Fletcher told me I could rise if I wished. I know about the marriage.' He seemed reluctant to put her down, she could feel his heart pump beneath her hand. 'I shall not swoon, I'm perfectly well, Ralph.' Her gentle reminder prompted him to stride into a small chamber and lower her gently to a sofa.

'I shall fetch you something to revive you.'

The door closed softly behind him; the room felt empty without his presence. She drew her feet under her; resting her head on the padded back she closed her eyes trying to make sense of the astonishing information that she was not, and never had been, married to Rupert.

Her heart skipped a beat. She was free. Ralph had called her sweetheart. Sarah was certain he felt the same as she. The information was too much to take in.

Thinking of her erstwhile husband brought home to her the enormity of his behaviour. She had agreed to go and live with him, be recognised as his lawful wife; if she had done so when they were not married she would have been beyond the pale.

She sighed, and stretched out her legs; her bruised foot was decidedly uncomfortable squashed beneath her. The crackle of the sweet smelling logs on the nearby fire was relaxing, she felt herself drifting away and sat up shaking her head to clear it.

It would never do to fall asleep where she was. She should go immediately to her own chamber, but a strange lethargy was pinning her to the sofa. For some reason she couldn't find the energy to stand. It had been a confusing morning and her head ached, perhaps it would not matter if she dozed for a few minutes.

Ralph spoke briefly to his mother,

ordered refreshments to be fetched but Grace had gone — the room was empty. Then he saw her stretched out on the sofa sound asleep. His breath caught in his throat. She was so beautiful, so perfect in every detail.

He strolled across and sat opposite, deciding he would wait until she woke. He got up to fetch a warm comforter, one his mother used on occasion, and gently draped it over her. Then he resumed his position, quite happy to spend the rest of the day gazing at the woman he intended to marry at the earliest possible opportunity.

How could he have fallen in love so quickly? He was about to retreat as quietly as he had arrived when her eyes flickered open. When she saw him she was radiant, her smile etched itself on his heart.

Grace saw his expression change from tender to something else entirely. His eyes darkened, his shoulders tensed and he leant towards her. He didn't move, he was waiting for her signal. Her head told her to remain aloof, then her arm moved of its own volition, her hand open towards him. In one bound he was beside her, dropping to his knees.

'My darling, I know I should not, but I cannot help myself. It has been torture for me standing back and allowing Rupert to be with you. Thank God there's no barrier, legal or otherwise, to prevent us being together.'

His eyes burned into hers, she was held captive by his ardour, could scarcely catch her breath. Her hands slowly came up to frame his cheeks. Her fingers traced the outline of his jaw, his bristles prickled her fingertips, his skin as hot as his eyes.

Slowly he closed the distance between them. She was mesmerised, her heart pounding, knowing that they were breaking every role of etiquette, but still she couldn't stop herself.

His arms reached around her waist and she was lifted from the sofa crushed to his heart. His mouth closed over hers. Nothing had prepared her for the intensity of feeling this kiss provoked.

Then she was rudely dropped back on the sofa and he was standing behind a chair. What was wrong? Had her wanton behaviour offended him? She felt as though a bucket of icy water had been tossed over her.

'Darling, don't look like that. I took shameful advantage of you, my only excuse is that I love you to distraction, and these past few days have thought of nothing else but having you in my arms. I believed I would never have the right.'

'Don't apologise, my love, you would not have come to me if I hadn't invited you.' She smiled at him teasingly. 'Are you not going to ask me if I reciprocate your feelings?'

His shout of laughter defused the tension. 'Devil take it! I should hope that you do, sweetheart, or I have sadly misjudged the situation.'

Grace patted the space beside her encouragingly. 'Then, my love, come and sit next to me.'

'My darling girl, make me the happiest of men. Do me the inestimable honour of becoming my wife.'

'I am delighted to accept your kind offer, my lord. Now kindly get up off your knees and stop making a cake of yourself.' He straightened and sat beside her, taking her hands in his. Hers looked so small inside his grasp. She raised her eyes to meet his tender gaze. 'Are we run mad to do this after such a short acquaintance? How do we know we will suit?'

'Do you love me? I've yet to hear those words from you.'

'I love you, Ralph, but I can't think why as you're the most overbearing, high-handed gentleman I've ever come across.'

He pulled her hands to his mouth and gently kissed each fingertip in turn before answering. 'And you, my darling, are the most aggravating, argumentative, headstrong young lady I've ever come across.' His smile made her toes curl. 'Therefore we are ideally suited.'

'I should like to be married in June. It's April now, so that should allow us ample time to get to know each other better before we say our vows.'

A discreet cough from the direction of the door jerked them apart. Sarah dabbed her eyes with a miniscule cotton square. 'My dears, I can't tell you how pleased I am to see that you have wasted no time in declaring your feelings.' Her comment made it quite plain that for some reason she disapproved.

He gave her hand a warning squeeze and then rose smoothly to his feet bringing her up with him. 'Mama, you should be the first to congratulate us. Grace has agreed to marry me. I'm sure we have your full support and approval, do we not.' The warning in his voice was quite unmistakable.

'Of course you do. I'm sure Rupert will offer his sincere congratulations as well.'

Grace felt wretched. She should have spoken to her first before accepting

Ralph's proposal. Had she inadvertently betrayed the trust Sarah had placed in her? If Ralph hadn't kept his arm firmly around her waist she would have run to Sarah's side.

'Rupert has nothing to do with this.' He smiled his special smile at Grace. 'Although I shall be eternally grateful to him for introducing us. If it hadn't been for his outrageous behaviour we would never have met.'

No, she would comfort her friend. She stepped out of his grasp and walked smartly across the salon. If she allowed him to dictate her behaviour so soon in their relationship then a precedent would be established. They would be constantly at daggers drawn because one thing she did know, she had no intention of being a subservient wife.

'Sarah, my lady, we discussed this earlier. You know Rupert and I would never have made a true match of it. I think of him as a dear brother. Both you and Ralph wanted me to persuade him to join the army. This debacle has produced exactly the result you wanted.'

Ralph strolled over to join them, he gave her a dark look. No doubt he would wish to take her to task when they were private. 'Also, you will recall telling me, Mama, not to despair as matters would resolve themselves in my favour. I don't understand why you are so reluctant to celebrate with us.'

Sarah stuffed her handkerchief into her reticule. 'I know it's quite irrational, but I hoped when this business with Rupert was resolved I would have Grace to myself for a few months at least before being banished to the Dower House.'

Grace flung her arms around her friend. 'You shall not move out of this house unless you wish to. Perhaps when it is overrun with the patter of little feet you might find it more peaceful elsewhere, but until then I should be bereft without your companionship.'

Too late she realised it was not her

decision to make, but her future husband's. Yet again she had spoken out of turn. She spun to face him, expecting to see a look of disapproval on his face. Instead his smile was the widest she'd ever seen.

'I can see I shall have my work cut out to be master in my own home in future with you two forming a coalition against me.' He chuckled and shook his head in mock despair. 'Now I shall be obliged to live with the two women. How shall I bear such a hardship?'

'Go away, you aggravating boy, dearest Grace and I have a wedding to plan.'

'I'm considering sending to London for a special licence . . . ' he began, having winked outrageously at Grace.

'You'll do no such thing, Ralph. We shall have the banns called in the village church as all our family have done for generations.'

'Sarah, he is funning. We have agreed we shall be married in June.' She dared him to contradict and he chuckled and raised both hands in surrender.

'There, Mama, plenty of time to do everything necessary.' He waved his acknowledgement and strolled off.

Grace thought him the handsomest man alive; and also the kindest and most considerate. Certainly it would not be a peaceful marriage, but it would never be boring, that was for sure.

'Thank the good Lord he is gone; Now we can start our planning; we have hardly long enough to arrange a wedding breakfast, send out invitations, and complete your new wardrobe. However, if we have only two months then we must make do with that.'

★　★　★

Grace spent the next few days closeted with Sarah discussing wedding plans, but each time the door opened she looked up hoping to see Ralph. 'Sarah, my head is spinning with all the names of people I'd never heard of who must be invited to the wedding breakfast.

Pray excuse me if I leave you to your lists for a while, I wish to stretch my legs.'

Her future mother-in-law looked up, her expression distracted. 'Yes, dearest girl, you run along and find Ralph.'

She emerged into the hall to see him striding towards her.

Quite ignoring Foster and two footmen he opened his arms and she walked in. She breathed deeply, loving his aroma of lemon-scented soap, horses and masculinity.

'Grace, sweetheart, I was coming to find you. I've just received a letter by express, I have to go to London urgently on business.'

'Will you be away long?'

'Two nights, no longer I promise you. It's the start of the Season, it will be heaving in town.' The look of disgust on his face made her giggle.

'I suppose being in London could be acceptable. After all there's the theatre, the opera, museums and lectures to attend. It needn't all be overheated ballrooms.' He grinned and touched her cheek. 'Next year we can hold a ball of our own if you wish.'

'Thank you, but I would much rather stay here with you in the country.'

'Don't let Mama wear you out, darling. Having remained stationary for three months she appears to be making up for the lost time. Your presence has energised her, she will run you ragged if you don't stand firm.' He pressed a kiss on her lips and stepped back, his eyes tender. The crunch of wheels on gravel reminded them the carriage was waiting in the turning circle.

'Take care, Ralph. I shall be lonely without you.'

'I shall be back before you have time to miss me. Mama will have you out on morning calls tomorrow and no doubt the next day as well. What with seamstresses, waiting lists and writing invitations you won't have a minute to spare.'

Ralph's valet appeared with his topcoat, he held it out and Ralph shrugged it on.

'I say, Ralph, wait for me, I'm coming to town with you. Might as well apply in person to Horse Guards.' Rupert bounded down the stairs, his valise in his hand, hotly pursued by Evans waving a topcoat and hat.

They walked to the carriage conversing amicably. She knelt on the window seat in order to see Ralph leave. He turned with one boot on the carriage step and waved to her, then tossed his hat and bag ahead of him and jumped in; Rupert bounced after him.

She had no wish to enter the salon and face the endless lists so chose to return to her rooms, change into her boots and take a stroll around the ornamental lake. On pushing open the door to her sitting-room she discovered two unfamiliar chambermaids putting the furniture under holland covers. They curtsied in tandem but renamed mute.

'Kindly tell me what's going on here.'

The taller of the two girls bobbed again. 'It's like this, Miss Hadley, his lordship said you must be moved to the Butterfly Suite. It's the grandest apartment.' The girl smirked at her partner. 'It's where the old master used to sleep.'

Grace guessed word of their betrothal had filtered downstairs to the servants' quarters. The maids vanished with a flick of their aprons through a door concealed in the panelling.

She had no idea the whereabouts of her new chambers and was about to ring for assistance when Molly bustled in. 'Well I never. Ever so smart where we've been moved, miss. I've made sure that all your gowns and such have been carried carefully, but even with so many your new closets are only half full.'

'I take it my good news is common knowledge downstairs?'

Molly nodded, beaming happily. 'Yes, miss, only the mistress ever sleeps in here.'

'Lord Shalford and I shall be married in June. I can't believe how happy I am. Shalford Hall is overlarge, but no doubt

I shall become accustomed to its size in time.'

The Butterfly Suite was everything one would expect of a master apartment to be. From the enormous bed with heavy silk hangings to the finest carpets and furnishings; nothing had been overlooked. The décor was old-fashioned, the chamber obviously not redecorated in Ralph's lifetime, but everything smelled fresh and clean and she was delighted to have been given this honour.

The remainder of the day she spent with Sarah examining swatches of materials which Madame Ducray had left on a previous visit. 'As Lady Shalford you will require far more clothes than you would have needed as plain Miss Hadley. Ralph has very deep pockets indeed, and will expect you to be dressed in the latest fashions.'

Grace retired to her magnificent new abode after dining quietly with Sarah in her rooms. She was reminded as she left that they were to pay morning calls on the neighbours the next day. This meant she must be back from her ride, bathed and changed and ready to leave at noon. Foster had been informed they would not dine downstairs until the gentlemen returned from London.

Two further riding habits had been ordered, but until then she must make do with the one she had. Promptly at seven thirty she appeared in the stable yard but was surprised to find Silver Star was not saddled and waiting for her. A stable boy tumbled down the stairs that led from the men's sleeping quarters, twisting his cap nervously in his hands.

'Beggin' your pardon, ma'am, but we ain't expecting you this morning. His lordship said as you wouldn't be riding whilst he was away.'

'There has been some misunderstanding. Saddle Silver Star immediately please. I intend to ride every day whether Lord Shalford is here or not.' She hated being stern with the boy, but if she wanted to override Ralph's high-handed decision she must be as autocratic as he.

The boy set to with alacrity and in no time at all the mare was ready. Grace led the horse to the mounting block and swung on to the saddle. How strange to find no other grooms in the yard. 'Billy, isn't it?' The urchin nodded vigorously. 'Why are you alone?'

'The men are eating their breakfast, ma'am, the horses are fed and watered, no need for them to be here if no-one is going out.'

Grace was accustomed to riding without a groom in attendance so didn't hesitate to set off unaccompanied. She had no intention of leaving the estate, would take the same route she and Ralph had ridden more than once.

After an exhilarating couple of hours she turned the mare and retraced her path. She would have a leisurely canter and then walk her horse until the animal was cool. She was not one to return her mount sweating and in distress. As she approached the entrance to the estate, the gatekeeper was about his business letting in a smart blue travelling carriage. She cantered back to the yard intrigued to know who the occupant was.

This time the yard was busy with grooms going about their daily business. Two grooms rushed forward to help her dismount. She hurried into the house intending to go upstairs and change before venturing down to discover who had arrived. However as she crossed the vestibule she recognised the voice raised in the grand salon.

Her throat tightened. Perspiration trickled down her spine. Sir John had found her and come to snatch her back and Ralph was not here to protect her. If she locked herself in her chambers she would be safe for he would not have the temerity to storm upstairs and drag her out. Her temper flared; this man would not bully her ever again and he was certainly not going to berate Sarah as he was if she had anything to do with it.

She squared her shoulders, said a quick prayer, and marched, head high to do battle with the man who had made her life miserable these past three years. She almost changed her mind when she saw he was not alone. He had a dark-garbed man beside him and two burly servants.

'Good morning, Sir John, to what do we owe this unexpected pleasure?' She adopted her most haughty pose, matching him glare for glare. Her gaze travelled disdainfully from his boots to his head as if he were a man of no account and not a person she feared. He was transformed from a commanding figure to a stout middle-aged man with receding hair and bloodshot eyes.

Emboldened, she stalked into the room and smiled calmly at Sarah. 'Lord Shalford, my future husband, is presently away on business, but he will be back tomorrow morning if you would care to return then.'

'Don't give me any of your impertinence, young lady! I'm still your legal guardian and I've come to take you back where you belong. I have the law on my side you know. You will come with me willingly or not, I care not either way.'

Her bravado slipped away. He was quite right, until she was either married or age twenty-five he had control of both her person and her fortune. Sarah must not be forced to endure any unpleasantness. Perhaps it would be best if she went without argument?

'Do not go with him, dear girl, I shall ring for assistance.' Sarah made a move towards the bell strap but one of the thugs intercepted pushing her roughly to one side. She fell heavily, crying out as she hit the floor.

'Sarah, let me help you.' She ignored her step-father and gently lifted her friend on to a chair. She spoke softly so not to be overheard. 'This will end badly if I don't go with him. Send word to Ralph by express when I'm gone.'

'Enough of this time-wasting, girl, your future husband is not Shalford but

Mr Bennett and he is awaiting you eagerly at Hadley Manor.'

'I cannot come without my belongings and my abigail.'

He scowled and pointed a stubby finger at Sarah. 'This one stays with my men. Any funny business from you and it will be the worse for her.'

How could this be happening? Sir John and his minions were behaving like something out of the worst kind of romance novel. If she was not so frightened she would find the situation farcical. For a moment she was tempted to refuse, to call his bluff, but Sarah was ash pale and rubbing her back as if she had re-injured her damaged spine. Grace daren't risk anything further happening.

'I shall be as quick as I can, Sarah. Please don't worry, I shall come to no harm.'

'Don't think to raise the alarm, missy. No-one can get in here and her ladyship remains right where she is.'

Grace straightened and glared at

him. 'If you harm her Lord Shalford will kill you. I give you my word I will accompany you without a fuss, so why don't you allow Lady Shalford to return to her apartment?'

'Very well, but I shall come with you.'

In the short time she had been away from Hadley he'd changed and not for the better. Although physically he appeared diminished in her eyes, somehow he appeared more dangerous. Something had happened to turn him from a blustering bully to a wicked villain.

Far safer to follow his orders if it meant Sarah would be safe. Ralph was no more than a few hours hard riding from Shalford — word would reach him later today. Knowing she would be rescued the next day, and what fate awaited Sir John, was enough to stiffen her spine.

'Come along, Sarah, we must do as he says. I shall take you upstairs. You must promise to remain where you are until we have left. I shall come to no harm, after all, am I not the golden goose?'

Nothing further was said as she assisted the trembling woman up the staircase. Her step-father walked directly behind them, his stench of stale sweat made her stomach churn. She waved away the footman who stepped forward. 'Thank you, but I can manage. Lady Shalford is feeling a trifle under the weather. Sir John is here to help.'

The servant stood aside and Sarah stumbled into her apartment. She called as she entered. 'Molly, we are to leave immediately. My trunks must be packed and ready in a quarter of an hour.'

Sir John was behind her. 'I shall wait here, don't think to run away.' He shook her arm and she flinched. 'I am your sole beneficiary, girl, remember that. If anything should happen to you your money comes to me.'

Her knees all but buckled beneath her. He must be desperate indeed to make such a wild threat. Should she risk calling for help? She'd given her word to accompany him without a fuss, but surely promises could be broken when made under duress?

'Don't call out — remember my men with Lady Shalford.' He released her arm and vanished into the passageway. She had missed her chance and must now do as he said.

In less than the allotted time, footmen were carrying her trunks to the waiting carriage.

'I am ready, sir. Shall we depart?' Her voice was commendably steady and she managed to smile at Sarah.

He nodded, his mouth tight. 'In which case, we will go.' Molly was hovering anxiously at the top of the stairs. 'Back to your work, girl, you will not be travelling with Miss Hadley.'

Before she could protest, he placed a pudgy hand in the small of Grace's back and all but pushed her down the stairs in front of him. Finally the butler realised what was taking place and, supported by two of his footmen, he surged forward to intervene

The rough men who had accompanied Sir John waved their cudgels and this was enough to deter the rescue attempt. Moments later Grace was bundled into the carriage and he and his lawyer piled in behind her. The coach rocked as his thugs scrambled on top.

'Ah! Now I have you, you Jezebel. Be glad Bennett is still prepared to marry you after your exploits these past weeks.'

Ignoring his outburst she slid across the seat and grabbed the door handle. Too late — a blanket was tossed over her head muffling her cries. Before she could untangle her arms or aim a kick in his direction a rope was twisted around her.

'Be still, or it will be the worse for you. Thought you could run out on me, did you? No-one gets the better of John Radcliffe, I can tell you.'

There was no point in struggling. If she lay still maybe he would remove the cloth from her head. The course material stuck to her mouth and nose. She couldn't breathe. She was suffocating.

Grave Danger

Ralph stretched out his legs enjoying the extra space, glad they had decided to dispense with their valets for this brief trip. 'Well, little brother, are you still determined to join the cavalry?'

'No other corps will do for me. I think I'll look quite the dandy in scarlet regimentals, don't you?'

'We must purchase you a pair of decent horses.' He grinned. 'You could take Caliban if you like.'

'No, thank you! He'd have me off in a trice, and well you know it. He's a brute of a beast, far too big for me.'

'In which case, Rupert, go to Tattersalls and select your own mounts. Send the bill to me. Whatever you need, you shall have it.'

He closed his eyes and settled back to doze for the remainder of the journey. Much as he loved his sibling he had no wish to make small talk for the next few hours. His brother slumped heavily in his own corner and soon the carriage was quiet.

He let his mind drift back over the past few weeks. It was scarcely credible he hadn't known the woman he loved until then. He sent up a heartfelt prayer of thanks to the Almighty for the miracle that had brought Grace into his life.

A loud snore jerked him from his reverie. Leaning forward, he stretched out and poked his brother sharply in the shoulder in the hope that it would stop the racket. His unexpected jab caused Rupert to fling out his arms. His brother's clenched fist ricocheted off the squabs connecting painfully with his nose.

'God's teeth! Watch what you're doing, you nincompoop.' Blood dripped copiously from his injury and he searched frantically for his handkerchief to stem the flow. Rupert lurched to his feet to offer assistance.

The carriage tipped alarmingly sending them into a melee of arms and legs in the well of the vehicle. This sudden transference of weight unbalanced the coach and it veered to the left, causing a wheel to lodge in the ditch at the side of the road.

Ralph swore volubly. 'Keep still, Rupert, we're making it worse floundering around like this.' Ralph carefully extricated himself from his brother's clasp and shouted to his coachman. 'Get down and see to the horses. We'll be out to help you in a moment.'

'I say, just look at my shirt? You've bled all over it,' Rupert complained. 'I only brought one clean for tomorrow when I visit Horse Guards.'

'Get it laundered. Now, help me open the door. We must get out to see if we can right this vehicle or neither of us will be going to London.'

Eventually the horses were untangled from their traces and the carriage back on the road. 'It's a damnable nuisance, Rupert, but I fear we will have to walk to the hostelry. The rear axle is cracked and our weight inside will snap it clean through.'

His brother shrugged. 'It's a fine day, and no more than a mile. The exercise will do us good. I need to be fit to be a cavalry officer.'

Ralph chuckled. 'I doubt this walk will make much difference. However, the fact that you have sworn off alcohol and gambling will definitely be beneficial to your health and my pocket.'

He turned to his coachmen who were busy re-harnessing the animals. 'I expect we will be there before you, I'll endeavour to find a wheelwright so the repair can be made speedily.'

The inn, a well-known stopping place for travellers, was bustling with ostlers taking care of horses and folk waiting to board the next mail coach. Rupert pointed to the group.

'Shall we catch the stage? It might be several hours before we can get our own carriage repaired.'

'I doubt we'd get a seat and I have no

intention of travelling on the top. I've heard of passengers freezing to death up there. We'll wait; although we both wish to get our business done there's no real urgency.' He gestured to an ostler who hurried over tugging his forelock.

'Yes, m'lord, can I help you?'

'My carriage has met with an accident and needs the rear axle repairing immediately. My coachman's bringing the vehicle here and will be arriving momentarily. Do you have a wheelwright available?'

The man nodded vigorously. 'We have our own forge and workshop out the back. I'll show your man where to take the coach when he arrives. I reckon if it ain't too bad it'll be done in an hour or two.'

Ralph tossed the man a coin which he caught deftly in a grubby hand. 'Come along, Rupert, we must find ourselves a chamber and get cleaned up. We might as well order refreshments whilst we're here.'

As always he had to stoop to avoid

braining himself on the door frame. Inside was as busy as the yard. This was one occasion when he was grateful for his height; the innkeeper could not fail to notice him glowering over the heads of those waiting for attention. The landlord recognised quality when he saw it.

He pushed his way through the throng and bowed.

'I see you have met with an accident on the road, sir. I have a splendid chamber with a private parlour and can send hot water up to you directly.'

The parlous state of their clothes and his blood spattered face had had the desired effect. 'Thank you. I also require something to eat. Does this establishment serve coffee, by chance?'

'It does, I shall have a tray brought to your room. We have a tasty venison pie, cold cuts, vegetable potage and freshly baked bread and various pastries.'

Rupert cut in. 'Lord Shalford has a prodigious appetite — send it all. Can you get our shirts laundered and pressed before we leave?'

'Leave it to me, sir. If you hand the soiled garments to the maid she will bring them down. We have a fine fire going in the scullery.' He snapped his fingers and a maid in a voluminous apron appeared at his side. 'April, run along and fetch hot water. Sammy, you take the gentlemen's bags and show them to their chambers.'

The urchin snatched up the bags and headed for the staircase that ran up the wall at the far side of the vestibule. He stopped outside a substantial door and flung it open with a flourish. 'Here you are, my lords, plenty of room for the both of you. The girl will be up in a moment with the hot water.'

Ralph followed him into the bed-chamber and was pleased with what he saw. Everywhere looked clean, the furniture polished to a high shine and not a cobweb in sight. 'Put the bags on the wash stand, lad, and go and help bring up the water.'

A second coin changed hands and

the boy skipped off, delighted with the transaction.

'Pity Evans isn't here. I won't get my neck-cloth right without his help.'

'Good grief! Can you not tie your own cravat? Time you learned to fend for yourself — you'll not have a valet scrambling after you in a few weeks.

Three quarters of an hour later Ralph was devouring a substantial meal and his brother, having finished considerably earlier, was lounging against the window frame watching the to-ing and fro-ing of the carriages.

'Devil take it! That's your livery on the groom who's just galloped into the yard.'

Cutlery clattered to the floor as Ralph shoved back his chair and strode to the window. Sure enough, tumbling from the saddle was one of his men. There could only be one reason for this unexpected arrival, something catastrophic had occurred Shalford Hall.

'Grab the bags, Rupert and follow me down.' Not waiting to see if his orders were followed he hurtled into the corridor and took the stairs three at a time. The groom was in the process of handing over his exhausted horse and claiming a fresh mount. His face was mud streaked, he looked ready to drop.

'George, are you looking for me?'

The man straightened and his fatigue vanished. 'My lord, I can't believe it. I thought I would need to ride another hour or two before I caught you.'

'What is it? What's happened?'

'Miss Hadley has been taken by Sir John Radcliffe. He burst into the house and threatened her ladyship so Miss Hadley decided it best to go with him.'

'Miss Hadley taken? We must hire mounts and get after Radcliffe.' Rupert clutched Ralph's arm, his face devoid of colour.

'I doubt they have anything up to my weight here. You take one of the team, they all go as well under saddle as harness.' Ralph ground his teeth. He didn't want to send his brother alone, but he had no choice. Until he could find an animal big enough he must let Rupert take the lead. 'Do you know where Hadley Manor is?'

'It's in Hertfordshire about twenty miles from St Albans. I wish I had my pistol, I fear it might be needed before this business is finished.'

George beamed and pointed to the saddle bags that had just been removed from his sweating horse. 'In there, my lord. Her ladyship sent weapons for you.'

'Take care, little brother. I shall be right behind you.'

He watched his brother gallop off, the coachmen thundering behind.

'Ostler, where can I buy a decent horse round here?'

The man removed his cap to scratch his bald pate. 'Don't rightly know, my lord. Reckon you could ask Fred, the farrier, he'd know if anyone has brung in a big one.'

Ralph shouldered his way through the grooms and followed his nose. The smell of burning hoof was unmistakeable. The blacksmith was a burly man; his massive forearms bulged as he hammered a horse shoe to fit a waiting horse.

'I need to purchase a decent mount — one that will carry me thirty miles without breaking down.'

The man glanced up and nodded but didn't stop his task. 'You could try Squire Norton, he's not far short of your weight. Not as tall, mind you.' He nodded at a sweating youth. 'Jonnie lad, show this gentleman the way to the Manse.'

'Well, lad, where does this Squire Norton live?'

'It's a good distance if you go by the road — but I'll take you across field, it ain't far that way.'

Once they were in the open country the lad was obliged to run to keep up with him. Taking pity on the boy Ralph slowed his pace. 'Do you know the horses in Squire Norton's stable?'

'I do that, my lord. I reckon Bruno

would suit you a treat. The squire don't take to him — the beast's a mite hard to handle. Has had him off a time or two.'

'Sounds ideal. Ah! Is this the entrance?' He had reached the entrance to a substantial red brick dwelling quite recently constructed.

Ralph ran the remaining distance but slowed his pace before entering the stable yard. It was immaculate, a dozen glossy heads bobbed over loose box doors. He smiled, pleased this establishment didn't stable their animals stalls inside the barn as many did. His sudden appearance caused a stable boy to drop his fork full of manure.

A tall man in neat brown breeches and checked shirt cuffed the lad. 'Stupid boy — sweep it up.' The blow was affectionate and caused merriment rather than concern.

'How can I help you, sir?' The head groom bowed and waited politely.

'I'm Lord Shalford. Your boy directed me here to buy a beast called Bruno.

My carriage has a broken axle and I have most urgent business in Hertfordshire. Is the horse for sale?'

'Most definitely, my lord. The master dislikes the animal but its nature is well-known in the neighbourhood so there has been no interest in his purchase. I warn you, Bruno is not an easy ride.'

Ralph nodded. 'No matter — if he's up to my weight and has stamina then I will buy him.'

Twenty minutes later the horse was saddled and Ralph was ready to leave. The gelding put his ears back tempted to take the lump out of him as he gathered up the reins. 'Enough of that, old fellow, I intend us to be firm friends before the end of this ride.'

He had been to St Albans once before, but today he would be taking a more direct route. If he kept sun behind him he would be going in the right direction. He dug in his heels, clicked his tongue, and set off at a gallop. Radcliffe was going to regret

his actions by the time he'd finished
with him.

* * *

When Grace came to the blanket had
been removed but her limbs were still
restrained. Her throat was sore, her
chest hurt and she desperately needed a
drink. She would not give her abductors the satisfaction of asking. She kept
her eyes closed, deciding it would be
preferable to be thought unconscious or
asleep than be forced to converse with
her captors.

'I don't like the look of her, Sir John.
She's far too pale. We should never have
covered her head like that and I think
we should remove the rope.'

'She's breathing and no longer
making that wheezing sound. She'll do,'
her step-father continued. 'I shall
remove her bonds when I'm certain
she'll not make another attempt to
escape.'

'As she's unconscious she can hardly

cause us further problems.'

'Be silent! I'll not have my orders questioned. I pay you more than enough to demand your obedience and loyalty.'

Sir John was obviously less sympathetic than his companion. Could she use this information to her advantage? When eventually she was released, might it be possible to appeal to the lawyer's better nature?

She had no idea how long she'd been in a swoon — it could have been an hour or a few minutes. The groom sent after Ralph and Rupert would travel faster on horseback than they could in their carriage.

Possibly rescue might be on its way already and her abductors about to meet their comeuppance. This happy thought raised her spirits and made the experience less dreadful. It also gave her the courage to confront her step-father.

She could not remain silent a moment longer. She twisted her head and opened her eyes. 'How dare you treat me in this way? Release me at once. You cannot coerce me into marrying your horrible friend and Lord Shalford is already on his way to punish you.'

Sir John recoiled and his cheeks flushed. The lawyer shrank back into the squabs.

'You have run mad to think you can get away with this. Even if I was unprotected you would still be brought to justice. You are disliked and reviled in the neighbourhood — no-one will support you.'

He sprung forward and struck her across the cheek. 'Enough from you, my girl. Shalford can do his worst, but he will be unable to prevent your marriage to Bennett. A special licence has been fetched and witnesses are waiting.'

He smiled, but it did not reassure her. 'Do you think me a simpleton? We will all swear you said your vows willingly. The certificate will be signed and you will be the wife of Bennett and we will both be wealthy men.'

Bile rose in her throat. Unless Ralph arrived before the ceremony all would be lost. He wouldn't hesitate to kill Bennett in order to release her and she couldn't let him do this. He would be arrested for murder and hanged. Her eyes filled. Whatever she had to endure, her beloved must remain a free man.

★　★　★

Bruno, once he understood what was required of him, settled down. Ralph was confident he'd made an excellent purchase. The animal was up to his weight and would carry him all day without flagging.

Massive hedges presented no obstacle; the gelding gathered himself and soared over with inches to spare. The miles vanished beneath the plunging hoofs. As a church clock struck mid-day Ralph turned into a roadside hostelry to rest his mount and find them both a much-needed drink.

He removed his gloves and used them to wipe the mud and perspiration from his face. A stable boy trotted out to take the reins of the sweating gelding. 'Walk him until he's cool then rub him down. Don't give him water immediately. Have him ready for me in half an hour.'

The boy grinned and stretched out to take the horse's bit. 'Yes, sir. It's been right busy this morning. There's a gentleman inside at the moment, he arrived not half an hour ago wanting the same thing.'

His wild ride across country had brought him up with Rupert. He marched into the inn. 'Ralph, I can't believe you're here already.' His brother rushed forward and embraced him. 'I'm ready to leave.'

'Stay. Far better that we arrive together.'

Rupert looked unsure. 'Surely it would be better if one of us was there as soon as may be? I'll leave at once.'

'No, wait for me. When our men are

mounted we can cut across country and will make far better time. I don't think Grace is in any immediate danger. Radcliffe is a fool to believe he can coerce her into marrying one of his cronies. She merely has to remain resolute until we arrive.'

Within the expected half an hour all four of them were mounted. Ralph patted Bruno's massive neck. 'Right, old fellow, we have another twenty miles to cover before you can rest.'

'That's a good horse. Can't believe you managed to find him so quickly.'

'Good fortune smiled on me. I shall take the lead, keep up as best you can.'

* * *

Each jolt of the carriage wheel as it bounced in a pothole sent spasms of discomfort down Grace's spine. She had been restricted to one position for too long. Surely they must stop for refreshments or at least to change the team?

'Sir John, please stop the carriage. I must use a retiring room immediately.'

The lawyer whispered. 'Sir John is asleep, Miss Hadley. If you give me your word you will not try to escape I shall release your bonds.'

'I promise. Your kindness will not go unnoticed when Lord Shalford arrives.'

He crouched beside her, there was little room in the well of the carriage and she was terrified her step-father would wake up before the knots were untied.

'There, I have done it. Wriggle your arms and legs to restore the circulation, but pray do it quietly.'

The carriage window was lowered and the blanket and ropes thrown out. She sighed. At least she could not be restrained again. The lawyer stuck his head out and attracted the attention of the coachman. By gesture alone he made his wishes clear and the carriage trundled to a standstill.

Grace held her breath. Sir John grunted but continued to snore. The door swung open and the steps were let down. Peabody indicated she get out.

'You must be quick, Miss Hadley, he could wake at any moment. The coachman will have to accompany you. I dare not let you wander in the woods alone.'

With averted face she headed for the densest clump of undergrowth she could see.

Five minutes later she scrambled back relieved and more comfortable. The door closed quietly, the coachman returned to his box and snapped his whip. They were once more in motion. Dare she risk a further whispered conversation with the lawyer?

'Mr Peabody, how much further is it before we need to rest the horses?'

'We won't be stopping, Miss Hadley. We're going directly to Mr Bennett's estate which is no more than five miles from here.'

Her stomach roiled. Ralph would go to Hadley Manor and couldn't reach her in time to prevent the wedding taking place. Sir John had deliberately misled her to make sure he was not found. Her life was over. She would rather be dead than married to Bennett.

⋆   ⋆   ⋆

'How much further, Ralph?' Rupert shouted as he reined back to look at a milestone.

'I don't know.' He beckoned to the coachman. 'Tom, there's a local in the field over there. Go and ask him the direction of Hadley Manor.'

Whilst he waited he dismounted and loosened Bruno's girth, indicating the others should do likewise. His exhausted gelding dropped his head and nibbled at the lush grass which grew in abundance along the edge of the lane.

'Don't know about your beast, Ralph, but my mare won't go much further. None of the carriage horses are used to such hard riding, and certainly not jumping the hedges and ditches that we have.'

'This horse is tired but there's another twenty miles in him.' He yawned and stretched.

The coachman trotted back and slid to the ground. 'My lord, you'll not believe what I've just discovered. A travelling carriage, exactly like the one Miss Hadley was put in, passed here not more than fifteen minutes ago.'

'Excellent. Is Hadley Manor far from here?'

Tom scratched his head. 'That's the puzzle, my lord, we are a good three hours from Hadley village. This lane won't take us there. I don't reckon Sir John's going home, not if he's travelling down this lane.'

'Blast! He must be taking her somewhere else. We must catch up with the carriage before we lose it.'

He had a bad feeling about this. Grace was in mortal danger, he just knew it.

★ ★ ★

The carriage picked up speed and lurched to one side. Her step-father woke up, stared at her, and his mouth twisted. 'Peabody, are you responsible for this?'

His fist bunched. He was going to strike the terrified lawyer. She must do something to intervene before the poor man was seriously injured. Without considering the consequences she threw herself across the carriage throwing Sir John backwards. His head cracked loudly against the door stunning him.

'Quickly, open the door. We'll never get another chance. Help me, if you wish to come out of this unscathed.'

Peabody scrambled over his employer and turned the handle. The door swung open crashing against the carriage. At any moment the coachman would rein back the team and all would be lost. The ruffians at the back must surely see what they were doing but she had no choice.

She put her shoulder against her step-father's back and pushed. 'Grab his arm, pull as hard as you can. Together we can tip him out.'

With a final desperate push her abductor was dislodged from the seat and vanished through the door.

Peabody had the sense to grab the strap and haul the door shut. Grace collapsed in a corner.

Unable to form a coherent sentence she closed her eyes and waited for her mind to clear. Slowly her breathing steadied and common sense returned. She sat up and straightened her spencer. 'Well, Mr Peabody, did you see where he landed?'

'I did, Miss Hadley, he fell into the ditch. I doubt he'll have suffered further injury.'

The carriage continued to travel at a canter. The coachman and the other villains had somehow failed to notice the ejection of their master.

'Something else has occurred to me, Mr Peabody. What will happen to Mr Bennett's children if he is arrested?'

He shook his head. 'Children? He's a

bachelor. That was one of Sir John's lies, what happens next, Miss Hadley? Removing Sir John is one thing, but I doubt Bennett will not be put off by his absence. The marriage will still go ahead and the witnesses still swear that you were willing.'

'But you will not. A ceremony conducted under duress is not legal, is it?'

'No, that's correct — it's not. I see where your thoughts are going. You intend to go through with the wedding and then have it set aside using myself as corroboration?'

'Indeed I do, sir.'

'I understand exactly. However, Lord Shalford does not know where we are and I doubt anyone at Hadley Hall will tell him. They are all in the pay of Sir John.'

'You do not know Lord Shalford. I can assure you he will obtain the information. How much further to our destination, do you suppose?'

'No more than a quarter of an hour I

should think. How are we going to explain the absence of Sir John?'

'I thought if I pretend to be in a swoon and you asleep they may assume he fell from the carriage without our knowledge.' Hardly a likely scenario but the only explanation she could think of that might do.

He looked dubious, as well he might. 'We have no alternative, Miss Hadley, so I will go along with your scheme. Wait, I have an idea that might help convince them.' He withdrew a length of twine from his pocket. 'I shall tie your hands and feet again.'

'What an excellent notion. Perhaps there might be another rug under the seat. Without that I'm sure those ruffians will see through our charade.'

The last knot was fastened around a second blanket just as the carriage turned in through the gates to Mr Bennett's mansion. 'There, Miss Hadley, you look more or less as you did before. You must feign a swoon and I shall pretend to be deeply asleep.'

He slumped into a corner and closed his eyes, pulling his hat down over his straggly grey hair. Grace did likewise, taking several steadying breaths. She could hardly pretend to be unconscious if her chest was heaving.

* * *

Bruno thundered around the sharp bend in the lane, sending clods of earth flying out behind him. 'Good boy, not much further now.'

The dust from the carriage still lingered between the hedges. Ralph raised his hand and sat back in the saddle. The gelding dropped from a gallop to a canter allowing Rupert and the grooms to catch up. All four horses steadied to a walk.

'They are just ahead of us. We must not arrive pell-mell, those villains might well be armed and I have no wish to receive a bullet through my head.'

'We shall complete the journey on foot. We can turn the horses into this paddock. With luck there will be fresh water somewhere in that field for them to find.'

The sun was sinking behind the distant trees. Dusk was the perfect time to mount his attack.

Ralph told his small band of men to keep to the shadows, make sure their faces were hidden inside their collars. The building to which Grace had been taken was substantial but not overly large. No more than a dozen windows gleamed in the setting sun. The roof was intact but the place had an air of neglect.

His jaw tightened. Radcliffe had sold his darling girl to the highest bidder. All involved in this atrocity would live to rue the day they had mishandled Grace and his mama.

*   *   *

The carriage rocked to a standstill and swayed as the two men alighted from the rear of the vehicle. Violent tremors rippled through Grace.

The door was wrenched open. 'Bloomin' hell! What's going on here?'

The lawyer played his part to perfection. 'Good Lord! Where is Sir John? Has he got out already?'

Grace groaned and opened her eyes. She screamed, pressing herself back into the squabs. The hideous noise had the desired effect and all three recoiled. The most repellent of the ruffians recovered first.

'Shut that racket, or it'll be the worse for you, missie.' He pressed a filthy hand across her mouth and she sank her teeth into it.

He swore and raised his fist to retaliate. She braced herself for the blow. Then, as if by giant hands, he was plucked from the coach and hurled aside like an unwanted toy.

'My darling, I have you safe, no-one shall ever hurt you again.' Two well-remembered hands grasped her and she was safe in his arms.

'Ralph, I can't believe it. I didn't

think you would reach me in time.' She wriggled, trying to free herself from the blanket so she could return his embrace.

'Hold still, sweetheart, I must cut the twine.' He delved into his boot top and removed a small dagger. 'I shall kill the man who dared to do this to you.'

'You must not hurt Mr Peabody. The lawyer helped me push Sir John from the carriage . . . '

'There, my love, you are free. Let me remove this blanket and then I can take you from the carriage.' Her previous statement finally registered. 'You did what? Grace, how did it happen?'

She was lifted from the seat and swung into the fresh air. Rupert greeted her as if he spent every day punching villains to the ground.

'Grace, I'm glad to see you well. I say, I've never had such a lark. That's everyone accounted for apart from Radcliffe. Where the devil is he?'

'We pushed him out of the carriage. You will find him somewhere, a few miles back.' She looked around anxiously for Mr Peabody, but he was nowhere to be seen.

'I love you. I just knew you would rescue me.'

He chuckled. 'You are an original, my darling, and I can see being married to you my life will never be dull.'

'Shall we go and find Radcliffe, Ralph, or clean up here first?'

'Go . . . ' Ralph's words were cut short as the crack of a rifle rent the air. Rupert clutched his chest and toppled to the ground.

Grace landed with a thump on the dirt and Ralph placed his hand firmly on top of her head and prevented her from rising. 'Stay down. One man with a rifle could kill us all.'

'Rupert . . . I must go to him. He was shot, he might die without my help.' His brother had fallen face down and wasn't moving. 'Please, Ralph let me go.'

He crouched beside her dropped his arm on her shoulders. 'No, sweetheart, it would be suicide. He wouldn't wish you to be harmed on his account.'

After the three shots no more had been fired. What the devil were they playing at? What did they hope to gain by killing any of them? She was right, someone ought to attend to Rupert or he could bleed to death.

'Tom, Fred, are you hurt?'

Scrabbling from beneath the carriage attracted his attention. He dropped to his knees and peered underneath. His coachman and groom inching their way towards him.

'We're fine, sir, only one bullet found its mark the other two are embedded in the carriage.' Tom elbowed his way through the dirt until his head was poking out. 'I saw the blighter that fired at us. Scruffy-looking beggar, an ex-serviceman, I reckon. Two smart middle-aged gents knocked the rifle aside and they've all gone into the house.'

'In which case, why are we lying on the ground? Are you quite certain the rifleman is no longer there?'

'Positive, my lord. That doesn't mean he's not got it pointed at us from a window.'

Grace was strangely quiet beside him. He glanced down. She was no longer there but beside his brother. He surged to his feet and flung himself down next to them.

She turned a tear-stained face towards him. 'He is still alive but his pulse is weak. Help me to roll him over.'

Together they grasped Rupert's arms and slowly turned him. A sick dread filled him.

Rupert's shirt was stained red and his face a deathly white. 'Quickly, help me rip up my petticoats. We must make a pad and bandages and attempt to stem the bleeding.'

Grace tried to sound confident, as if she knew what she was doing. She had once assisted the apothecary when a farmhand had sliced his shoulder open with a scythe, but that was the extent of her knowledge. She stepped out of her undergarment and tossed it to him.

Pressure must be placed on the wound, that much she did remember. 'The bullet must still be inside, for there is no exit wound on his back. That is far more dangerous than if it had gone right through.'

Ralph completed his task and handed her a wad of folded material and the torn strips. She closed her eyes and sent up a fervent prayer before ripping open Rupert's sodden shirt. Her eyes widened. 'Thank the good Lord, it's his shoulder that has been injured. I couldn't see clearly before because of all the blood.'

Moments later the makeshift bandage was in place and the bleeding stopped. 'We must find a doctor at once, Ralph. My ministrations will not do for long. The physician must dig out the bullet and suture the wound.'

'Tom, I don't care about the rifleman. Run to the house and demand the address of the nearest doctor. If whoever's in there had intended to kill us we would all be dead by now.'

Ralph's topcoat was now a makeshift pillow for his brother. With both pistols tucked into the top of his breeches he looked like a buccaneer. His expression was grim, his eyes like flint as he removed the weapons, cocked them and held one out to her.

'Take this, sweetheart. I doubt you'll need it, but it's best to be prepared. Do you know how to use it?'

She nodded. Her throat was clogged with unshed tears. From triumph to disaster in the space of seconds — why had this happened?

'Good girl. Stay with Rupert, keep him calm. I'm going to the house with Tom and Fred.' He stepped away then looked around frowning. 'Where is this Mr Peabody? You say he was on our side?'

She nodded. 'He must be hiding. He will not assist those in the house even if he doesn't help us.'

'Good, so long as he's not going to interfere. Fred bring your cudgel, it might well be needed.'

Grace smoothed Rupert's hair, pleased to discover his face was somewhat warmer than it had been a few minutes ago. He was a dear boy, she loved him as a brother and prayed he would not die from his injury.

'Miss Hadley,' someone called from behind a clump of rhododendron bushes. 'Is it safe to emerge? Are those men likely to wake up?'

She scanned the four inert figures who showed no sign of regaining consciousness. 'Mr Peabody, I'm so glad you're unharmed. I should be grateful for your assistance, I'm sure it is quite safe.'

The lawyer peered out from the branches. Slowly he pushed his way through and scuttled across the open space.

'I thought it best to absent myself, Miss Hadley. I would only have got in the way.' He mopped sweat from his brow before settling down in the shelter the carriage. 'I don't know who the rifleman is — he must be someone Mr

Bennett has employed. The other gentleman, the one wearing a plum-coloured topcoat, is Mr Forsyth, another friend of Bennett.'

'Lord Shalford has gone to the house. We must send for a doctor. I fear Mr Shalford will have to remain here until he's recovered.'

Her companion appeared to have recovered his aplomb as he smiled. 'That should be an interesting experience, Miss Hadley. I thought, perhaps, I should go around to the stable yard and arrange for a groom to ride for the physician.'

'Yes, do that, sir. I suppose we had better send the carriage back to find Sir John; although I would far prefer to leave him where he is.'

'I shall bring a coachman and a stable hand back with me and they can take the coach to look for him. I shall not be accompanying them. My employment with Sir John is over.'

He pulled himself upright and her heart went out to him. He looked aged beyond his years, a broken man, and despite his involvement with her step-father she was determined to help him.

'Mr Peabody, I shall ask Lord Shalford to employ you in future. When I am married I shall regain my inheritance and Hadley Manor will be mine once more.' This was not quite true, as in law it would all belong to Ralph, but she was certain he would give her full control of her ancestral estates. 'Your knowledge of Hadley will be invaluable in the transfer.'

He straightened and looked like his old self again. 'I don't deserve such compassion. However, if his lordship is gracious enough to give me that task I can promise you I shall not fail.' He leaned forward and whispered conspira-torially. 'I have knowledge of Sir John's nefarious doings, ledgers and such like. I will give them to Lord Shalford to use against my former employer.'

Her attention returned to the patient. He was certainly breathing more easily and his colour was less pale. She checked the bandage and was delighted to discover no further blood, her makeshift arrangement was doing its job.

The estate was strangely silent, no sign of any other servants, no shouting or running feet. Why was that? Also she had heard no banging on the door when Tom went to the house. She would risk standing up and looking for herself.

★   ★   ★

Ralph strode towards the house his shoulders rigid, expecting a bullet to kill him at any moment. The house was quiet — no sign of faces at the shutters or voices raised in anger. Tom hammered on the door but there was no response.

'Go around to the back — one of the staff will know where the doctor lives. Send a groom to fetch him and then return to me.'

His coachman nodded and disappeared down the flagged path that ran along the side of the house. Ralph lifted the heavy brass knocker and banged it several times. The door shook under the onslaught. 'Open the door. Unless you all want to be hanged as murderers?'

This time there was a reaction. Hesitant footsteps approached the door and a female voice wavered. 'Mr Bennett and Mr Forsyth have left the premises and the man responsible for firing at you has gone with them.'

'I don't give a damn about that. Get this door open at once, my brother is bleeding to death out here and I wish to get him into a clean bed.'

The rasp of the bolts being drawn back meant the woman, presumably the housekeeper, was opening the door. As soon as it moved he placed his shoulder against it and shoved, sending the unfortunate female staggering back against the wall.

'I beg your pardon, ma'am, but I had no wish for you to change your mind. My brother's life might depend on the next few hours.'

The woman recovered quickly and dipped in a deep curtsy. 'This is a bad business, sir, indeed it is. I shall get the room prepared immediately. Dr Adams lives only a mile away in the village. He's an excellent physician and well thought of in these parts.'

'Good. My coachman is already taking care of this. How many footmen do you have?'

'Three, and a butler. They refused to help so are locked in the root cellar. I've already sent a girl to release them. They can fetch a trestle and carry in the injured young man.'

He had better introduce himself and explain there would be three chambers required plus accommodation outside for Tom and Fred. 'I am Lord Shalford, my brother Rupert Shalford is a gentleman who has been shot. Miss Hadley, my betrothed, will also require accommodation and the girl to assist. Her trunks are on the carriage.'

'Jenkins, my lord. I shall be pleased to help you and your lady in this crisis.'

She spun her blue bombazine crackling as she moved. 'Oh dear! What shall I do with the curate hiding in the pantry?'

'Tell him to disappear. The fewer people here at the moment the better.' His lips twitched. He was issuing orders as if the master of this establishment. Too bad, when things needed doing there was no time to stand on protocol.

$$\star \quad \star \quad \star$$

'Ralph, I was becoming agitated by your absence. Rupert is a little better and the bleeding has stopped.'

'That's excellent news, sweetheart.' He knelt beside her, dropping a quick kiss on her brow before checking the information was accurate. 'The men are coming to carry him in. The housekeeper is preparing rooms for us all and the physician has been sent for. Bennett, Forsyth and the rifleman have fled.'

He slipped his arm around her waist and gently pulled her to her feet. Grace relaxed against him for a moment, his warmth gave her the strength she needed. 'This is such a muddle, If Bennett intended to marry me why did he have a rifleman inside the house?'

'I've no idea, my love, but I shall make it my business to find out as soon as I'm certain Rupert is out of danger. No-one harms those that I love and gets away with it.'

His eyes were like brown pebbles, his jaw rigid and she prayed he would not put himself outside the law when he came face-to-face with the perpetrator of this disaster.

Rupert was transferred to a trestle and transported into the house. It was an hour or more before Dr Adams had dealt with the injury and declared his patient in no danger. She and Ralph remained in the chamber, hardly daring to believe the crisis was over.

'Come, sweetheart, shall we sit over there? I have yet to hear the full account of what transpired today.' He took her hand and led her to the window, settling herself comfortably in the corner before he scooped her on to his lap.

Whilst she was speaking his chin rested on top of her head which was most distracting. She completed her tale and his arms tightened.

'Radcliffe will regret his actions. How dare he mishandle my mother?'

'Word must be sent to Sarah. I dread to think how she will react when she hears Rupert has been injured,' Grace said.

'You mustn't fret, sweetheart, my mama is more resilient than you realise. I expect she has already packed her trunk and is on her way to Hadley Manor as we speak.'

'But she will not find us there . . . '

'I shall send a groom over to Hadley later. She will not travel at the breakneck speed we did. I'm sure she will reserve a chamber somewhere en route.'

'I don't understand why Bennett should have hired a rifleman. Surely his intention was to marry me, so why would he wish to kill anyone?'

The sound of a carriage rumbling over the gravel attracted their attention. His body tensed and he swung his legs to the floor. 'Radcliffe has arrived. Remain here, Grace. I wish to speak to him alone.'

She scrambled from his lap, shaking the creases out of her travel weary gown. 'No, Ralph. I must be there. Whatever my step-father has done, let the law deal with him. I know how angry you are . . .'

His eyes darkened and his mouth thinned. He was going to refuse. Then he smiled and held out his hand. 'Very well. We shall speak to him together. We cannot leave Rupert unattended. Ring the bell — the housekeeper must sit here whilst we are away.'

Five minutes later the woman arrived, apparently unflustered by this sudden request.

She curtsied. 'I shall remain at the young man's side, my lord. I am experienced in such matters.'

Reassured, Grace smiled and hurried after Ralph who was already halfway down the stairs. She hesitated on the landing, not sure if she wanted to come face-to-face with her abductor, the man who had sold her to Bennett.

She expected to hear him blustering, demanding restitution for having been thrown headfirst from a moving carriage but she heard nothing apart from the shuffling feet of the two grooms who were escorting him.

As she watched from her vantage point a man she didn't recognise was half dragged, half walked, through the front door. The man who had bullied her these past years, who had been stealing her inheritance and ruining Hadley was no more. This broken wretch, his clothes in disarray, was no-one to be frightened of.

She slipped into the drawing-room unnoticed. Ralph stood, legs apart, hands clenched behind his back glaring at Sir John. 'Put him on that chair. I doubt he can stand unassisted.'

What Sir John told Ralph confirmed what she already knew. Her step-father had agreed to fetch her in return for half her inheritance and he was astounded to discover they had been fired at on their arrival.

'Lock him in a room somewhere. I shall not soil my hands on him. The magistrate can deal with his wrong-doing. Kidnapping is a capital offence, Radcliffe.' This was stated clearly, the meaning unequivocal.

Grace was about to ask for clemency on his behalf but Ralph shook his head slightly. She waited, not sure what to expect.

'I beg you, my lord, do not hand me over to the authorities. I will sign away all rights to Hadley Manor and the estate if you will let me go. I promise I shall go abroad and you will not hear from me again.'

Ralph appeared to think about it and then nodded. 'I believe there is a lawyer somewhere on the premises. I shall have the papers drawn up. Sign them before witnesses and then go.' He lunged forward, gripping the sides of the chair, placing his face inches from his prisoner.

Grace felt sorry for her step-father's final humiliation, but he should suffer for what he had done. A lesser man than her beloved might have beaten him within an inch of his life before tossing him into jail. This way Hadley would be returned to her and Radcliffe would be gone for ever.

She retreated to the entrance hall to discover the butler shifting from foot to foot. He was obviously waiting to speak to either Ralph or herself.

'My lady, I must explain to you what happened. Mr Bennett and Mr Forsyth decided they would take your inheritance for themselves. They hired an ex-serviceman to shoot Sir John when he arrived. He had been told to kill the two gentlemen with you in the carriage. Somehow in the confusion he mistook Mr Shalford and his lordship for the lawyer and Sir John.' He ran his hands as if he was personally responsible. 'When they realised what they'd done they fled. What will happen to them now? We shall all be in the poor house with no master to pay our wages.'

Ralph had arrived during this explanation and he answered the butler. 'I shall demand the estates of both Bennett and Forsythe in recompense. I give you my word none of you will suffer because of your master's perfidy.'

The elderly retainer scuttled off no doubt to relay the good news to the rest of the staff. Ralph's laughter broke the tension. 'I can't believe they thought to get away with such a cracked-brain scheme. They must all have been touched in the attic.'

The following day Sarah arrived, accompanied by Molly, and was remarkably unfazed by all that had transpired. She took over the sick room allowing Ralph to continue to London to complete the business that had been abandoned. On his return two days later they were gathered in the drawing-room.

'My dears,' Sarah said, 'I knew how it would be once Ralph was in charge of matters. My darling Rupert is making a remarkable recovery. I fear he will wish to go off to be a cavalry officer before his shoulder is fully healed.'

'I have given the matter some thought, Mama, and have, I believe a solution. I have already put the matter to Rupert and he is delighted with my suggestion.'

'What is it, Ralph? You have not discussed anything with me.' Grace frowned at him.

'I know, my love, but I did not wish to bother your pretty head with business matters.'

She drew breath to protest at his high-handed attitude but his chuckle forestalled her. 'No, don't poker up at me, my girl. I am the lord and master here, and I intend it shall remain that way.'

'Ralph, dear boy, do not tease. Tell us

277

at once what you and Rupert have devised.'

'I have signed over this property and also the Rookery, which was owned by Forsyth, to Rupert. He now has five decent estates to manage and his income will be substantial. Considerable work must be done to make them profitable again, but it is a challenge Rupert wishes to take on.'

'Thank you, my boy. It is exactly what Rupert needs to steady him. I do declare his being shot has turned out to be of benefit to us all.' She smiled lovingly at Grace. 'I shall leave you two together, for I must relieve the housekeeper who is sitting with Rupert.'

Sarah drifted past, no sign of her former infirmity apparent, patting her son on the back as she did so. 'I shall give you some privacy, dearest boy. I'm sure you have much to discuss.'

Grace felt her knees unexpectedly wobble. Then his dear arms were around her and she was lifted from her feet in a bear hug. She clung to him, her cheeks wet. He slowly lowered her but kept her pressed tight to him.

Ralph answered for her. 'Correct, Mama. Tell Rupert we will be along shortly.' He waited until the doors closed for a second time before sweeping her up in his arms and carrying her to the sofa where he sat, keeping her firmly on his lap.

'I love you, my darling. If any man comes within one hundred yards of you again I shall not be responsible for my actions. You are my life, my everything, I give you my word I shall keep you safe from harm.'

She supposed she should protest about the unconventional way they were sitting on Mr Bennett's sofa, but she was too happy, too comfortable to do so. 'It's hard to believe that our lives have been so changed. Rupert has become wealthy, my step-father has been sent packing, and you and I are to be married in June.'

He smiled lazily, sending unexpected shivers up and down her spine.

'Actually, sweetheart, we are getting married tomorrow. I have a special licence in my pocket. I refuse to wait any longer. And anyway, far better to return to Shalford as my wife after the harum-scarum way you departed.' He grinned. 'That curate is returning to perform the ceremony. He dared not refuse.'

His golden eyes burnt into hers and her breath caught in her throat. Slowly he lowered his head and his lips covered hers.

THE END

We do hope that you have enjoyed reading this large print book.

Did you know that all of our titles are available for purchase?

We publish a wide range of high quality large print books including:

Romances, Mysteries, Classics
General Fiction
Non Fiction and Westerns

Special interest titles available in large print are:

The Little Oxford Dictionary
Music Book, Song Book
Hymn Book, Service Book

Also available from us courtesy of Oxford University Press:

Young Readers' Dictionary
(large print edition)
Young Readers' Thesaurus
(large print edition)

For further information or a free brochure, please contact us at:
Ulverscroft Large Print Books Ltd.,
The Green, Bradgate Road, Anstey,
Leicester, LE7 7FU, England.
Tel: (00 44) **0116 236 4325**
Fax: (00 44) **0116 234 0205**

Other titles in the
Linford Romance Library:

THE FAMILY AT FARRSHORE

Kate Blackadder

After breaking up with Daniel, archaeologist Cathryn Fenton quite happily travels to Farrshore in Scotland to work on a major dig. In the driving rain, she gives a lift to Canadian Magnus Macaskill, then finds that they both lodge at the same place. The dig goes well, with Magnus filming the proceedings for a Viking series. But trouble looms in Farrshore — starting when Magnus learns that his son Tyler is coming over from Canada to be with his dad . . .